Blaze®

Dear Reader,

Welcome to another Sons of Chance summer! First up is the cowboy many of you have been asking about, Nash Bledsoe. Nash made an appearance in the epilogue of *Feels Like Home,* an August 2012 release. Some readers guessed that he'd play a starring role in the next book, and here he is!

Let me tell you a secret. I belong to a fabulous plotting group that includes Harlequin authors Rhonda Nelson, Kira Sinclair and Andrea Laurence. We meet twice a year to brainstorm. Usually the stories don't have titles yet, so we assign them a label. This one became known as the "burning recliner book," and you'll understand why by the end of the first chapter.

If I wrote something other than romance, like maybe thrillers or horror, you might get a burning recliner on the cover, because it's a significant part of the story. But luckily for you, I do write romance, so instead you get a yummy picture of Nash Bledsoe. Much better, huh? I knew you'd think so!

I Cross My Heart kicks off this year's installment of the series, and it'll be followed by *Wild at Heart* in July. Then *The Heart Won't Lie* comes out in August, and—bonus!—*Cowboys & Angels* will show up in December. Please do join me at the Last Chance Ranch, where the summers are cool, but the cowboys are extremely hot!

Yours for the summer and beyond,

Vicki

Vicki Lewis Thompson

—

I Cross My Heart

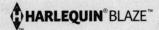
HARLEQUIN® BLAZE™

Recycling programs
for this product may
not exist in your area.

ISBN-13: 978-0-373-79755-4

I CROSS MY HEART

Copyright © 2013 by Vicki Lewis Thompson

Printed in U.S.A.

ABOUT THE AUTHOR

New York Times bestselling author Vicki Lewis Thompson's love affair with cowboys started with the Lone Ranger, continued through Maverick and took a turn south of the border with Zorro. She views cowboys as the Western version of knights in shining armor—rugged men who value honor, honesty and hard work. Fortunately for her, she lives in the Arizona desert, where broad-shouldered, lean-hipped cowboys abound. Blessed with such an abundance of inspiration, she only hopes that she can do them justice. Visit her website, www.vickilewisthompson.com.

Books by Vicki Lewis Thompson

HARLEQUIN BLAZE

To get the inside scoop on Harlequin Blaze and its talented writers, be sure to check out blazeauthors.com.

Other titles by this author available in ebook format.
Don't miss any of our special offers. Write to us at the following address for information on our newest releases.

Harlequin Reader Service
U.S.: 3010 Walden Ave., P.O. Box 1325, Buffalo, NY 14269
Canadian: P.O. Box 609, Fort Erie, Ont. L2A 5X3

To Edward Knabusch and Edwin Shoemaker, who invented the first wooden recliner in 1928 and made an upholstered version dubbed the La-Z-Boy in 1929. This story wouldn't be the same without that invention, so thanks, guys!

Prologue

June 18, 1982, Last Chance Ranch
From the Diary of Eleanor Chance

A BABY APPEARED ON OUR doorstep today. Not literally, but as good as. Nicholas Jonathan O'Leary, five months old, arrived in a taxi with his own personal lawyer as a temporary nanny.

Apparently fourteen months ago, my son, Jonathan, conceived this child with that flighty Nicole O'Leary, one of the women he attached himself to during what I call his yee-haw phase. She was only in town for a couple of months, and after she left, Jonathan didn't hear from her. Until this baby showed up.

According to the lawyer, Nicole had wanted Nicholas's existence to be kept secret while she was alive, but she'd arranged for him to be brought here in the event of her death. Good thing she made those provisions, considering she'd taken up skydiving! Who does that kind of thing when they have an infant to care for? I shouldn't speak ill of the dead, but, honestly! She had Shinola for brains, if you ask me.

Jonathan, of course, is shocked by her death and the baby he'd had no clue about. He also feels guilty for having unprotected sex with her. But Archie and I don't really blame him. He wasn't himself after his no-good wife, Diana, left him and their toddler, Jack, two years ago. Archie and I made sure that Jack was cared for during those months when Jonathan battled a sense of failure by painting the town.

Then, thank the good Lord, he met Sarah, and they had the loveliest Christmas wedding this past December. Sarah is everything Jonathan's ex-wife was not. She's a nurturing and loving presence in our lives and little Jack finally has a mother.

We've all been anticipating the birth of Jack's baby brother, Gabriel, due in four months, and now…well, Sarah says Jack will have two little brothers, Nick and Gabe. That tells you what my new daughter-in-law is made of. The angels smiled on us when she agreed to marry our son.

So, before you know it, Archie and I will have three grandchildren! Archie is over the moon about that. Jonathan will inherit the Last Chance Ranch when we're gone, and the odds are good that one of those boys will take over from Jonathan someday. Maybe they'll even share ownership. Wouldn't that be nice?

Archie feels very sentimental about keeping the ranch in the family. Today, in the midst of the hullabaloo about Nicholas arriving, Archie coined a name for Jonathan's boys, each with a different mother. He calls them the Sons of Chance. I think that's sweet.

1

WHEN IT CAME TO MENTAL health, Nash Bledsoe vastly preferred shoveling shit to lying on a therapist's couch. His newly minted ex-wife, Lindsay, felt differently and had told him numerous times he needed a shrink. But his final divorce papers had arrived from Sacramento late yesterday afternoon, and Lindsay no longer had any say-so about how he dealt with his emotions.

Now that they were officially divorced, he'd never again have to hear Lindsay quote her favorite self-help guru, Bethany Grace: Happiness Is a Choice. He shuddered. God, how he'd come to hate that phrase.

Well, damn it, today he chose to be mad as hell. And mucking out stalls was both productive and therapeutic. He wouldn't deny that he had plenty of issues, but fortunately the Last Chance barn had plenty of stalls.

"Better slow down before you hurt yourself, son."

Nash glanced up in midshovel. Emmett Sterling, the Last Chance's foreman, leaned in the doorway of the stall and chewed absently on a piece of straw. The guy looked more like a veteran cowboy than anyone Nash knew. Although he was past sixty, he had the lean body of a man much younger. His graying mustache gave him an Old West look that suited him.

"The exercise feels good," Nash said.

"I expect it does. Heard about the divorce papers arriving."

"Yep. I'm officially a free man." He didn't pretend to be surprised that Emmett knew. His mail was delivered to the bunkhouse, and his buddy Luke Griffin had been there when he'd opened the thick envelope.

Luke had worked at the Sacramento riding stables owned by Nash and Lindsay, but he'd lost his taste for the job when Nash had left. So Nash had put in a good word for him here at the Last Chance and Luke had hired on a couple months after Nash had. Last night Luke had joined him in polishing off a bottle of Wild Turkey, and several of the other hands had produced some twelve-packs and turned it into a party.

The divorce papers hadn't been a surprise. Lindsay had filed almost a year ago, and Nash had spent some time and money trying to get a fair shake. Turned out to have been a waste, and seeing the settlement spelled out in black and white had brought back all his suppressed rage. He tossed the shovelful of manure into the wheelbarrow and went back for more.

"I remember being as angry as you are right now. It'll pass," Emmett said.

Nash dumped more manure into the wheelbarrow. "Especially if I keep shoveling." He'd forgotten that Emmett's wife had divorced him twenty-some years ago. Now Emmett was seeing Pam Mulholland, who owned a bed-and-breakfast on the main road into town.

Pam was part of the Chance family through her late sister, Nicole O'Leary, mother of Nick Chance. A wealthy divorcée with no children, Pam had moved to the Jackson Hole area to be near her nephew. And she'd soon fallen head over heels for Emmett Sterling.

But Emmett was dragging his feet about marrying her because she was loaded and Emmett was not. Nash could relate. Lindsay's money had been a ticking time bomb—one he'd foolishly deemed unimportant when he'd asked her to share his life.

"I hate to interfere with your plan to work until you drop," Emmett said, "but one of the hands spotted a column of smoke over at the Triple G. I need someone to check it out, and I'm afraid you're nominated."

"Glad to." Nash was grateful to have a job and was committed to doing anything the foreman asked of him. He laid the shovel across the load in the wheelbarrow. "Just leave me some stalls to muck out, okay?"

"That can be arranged."

Emmett and Nash walked out of the barn, their booted feet making hollow sounds on the wooden floor. "It's bad enough that Hank Grace had to drink himself to death," Emmett said. "I hate to think of someone trespassing and starting a fire because nobody's around to stop them."

"Nobody's there?"

"Far as I know. Hank sold off the animals months ago. From what I heard, he abandoned the place and checked himself into a hospital in Jackson. Died there a week ago. Don't know what's supposed to happen with the property."

Nash had been gone long enough that his memory was cloudy when it came to some of the residents of this area. "Wasn't there a daughter?" He vaguely remembered that she'd been several years behind him in school.

"Yeah, but she turned into a city girl and wasn't around much. I doubt she's the one lighting a fire over there. Doesn't fit. Could be kids having a campout, but it's still trespassing, and I never like seeing unexplained smoke. Untended fires can spread." Emmett handed Nash a set of keys. "Take the Ford F-150. There's a fire extinguisher behind the seat. I'd rather not bring the sheriff into it if we don't have to, but you have your cell phone, right?"

"Yes."

"Call the law or the fire department if you can't handle it, but I'm hoping it's nothing too drastic."

"Probably isn't. School's out. Stuff happens."

"That's my thought. Thanks, Nash."

"You're welcome. See you soon." Nash tugged his hat a little lower over his eyes to block the glare of the bright June sunshine. He could see the smoke rising about five miles away.

Maybe this break would help rid his mind of depressing thoughts. He'd failed to create a happy marriage, and he wasn't used to failure. But at least his family and friends hadn't witnessed the debacle firsthand. He'd grown up in Jackson Hole, but he'd spent the past ten years in Sacramento, nine of them married to Lindsay.

He should have known when she'd asked him to sign a prenup nine years ago that no matter how hard he worked, he would never have been considered an equal partner in that riding stable. Her parents had constantly reminded him that they'd bankrolled the business and bought Nash and Lindsay a home, to boot.

Lindsay had never called them on that, either, and his relationship with her had started unraveling after the first year. Good thing his old friend Jack Chance had given him a job last fall. Nash had literally come out of the marriage with nothing but his truck, which needed a valve job.

He'd put that off because he seldom drove anywhere on personal business and he had use of the ranch vehicles when Emmett needed something done, like now. Food and lodging were part of the job. That allowed Nash to invest most of his salary, and thanks to a good financial adviser in Jackson, his savings were growing nicely. Eventually he'd have enough for a down payment on his own place.

The tan ranch truck was parked near the two-story main house. As he walked the short distance, he rolled his shoulders to ease the tension that had settled the moment he'd opened the envelope from Sacramento. He hated to think his life was spiraling downward, but sometimes it felt that way, especially when he compared his situation to Jack Chance's.

Jack was technically his boss, although he would never pull rank. They'd been friends since high school, where they'd been in the same graduating class and had played on the same football team. But now their situations were totally different.

Jack's dad had died several years ago in a rollover, leaving his three sons and his wife as joint owners of this valuable operation. The Last Chance bred paints and trained them as cutting horses. As the oldest son, Jack ran the daily operation in partnership with his mother, Sarah. Middle brother Nick was a vet with his own practice, but he made sure all the animals on the ranch stayed healthy. Gabe was the competitor who rode the Last Chance horses and showcased the ones offered for sale.

Sarah and her fiancé, Pete Beckett, lived in the main house, but each of the sons had staked out a parcel of ranch land and had built homes for themselves and their wives. No doubt about it—the Chance brothers had been blessed with good fortune. Nash didn't begrudge them any of it, but he longed for that kind of financial and emotional stability.

He was working to build up a nest egg now, but finding the right person to love would have to come later. He wasn't about to hook up with a woman until he had resources. He'd learned his lesson on that score. He'd already made one big mistake, and he wasn't planning to make another.

Climbing into the dusty ranch truck, he started the engine and backed the vehicle around. The long and tortuous dirt road that connected the ranch to a paved two-lane highway was always a challenge, but at least today it was dry. Jack's dad had deliberately left the road unpaved to discourage trespassers, and his sons had decided to honor that tradition.

A little bit of grading wouldn't hurt, though, Nash thought as the truck bounced over the hardened ruts. The ranch had a tractor and a blade, but apparently using it on the road would be considered sacrilegious. Nash wondered how often Jack had to replace the shocks in his trucks because of these ruts.

After a bone-jolting drive, Nash reached the two up-right poles and massive crossbeam that marked the entrance to the Last Chance. To the left, about ten miles away, was the little town of Shoshone. It supplied many of the basics, like food, gas and a great bar, the Spirits and Spurs, owned by Jack's wife, Josie. But for anything fancy, people had to drive nearly an hour into the city of Jackson.

Nash took a right toward the Triple G, a much smaller spread than the Last Chance. As Nash recalled, the Graces had kept to themselves—not a common thing around here, but it happened. Not all country folk were social.

Grace. He'd likely always cringe when he heard that last name now. His marriage had probably been doomed from the first day, since Lindsay's wealthy parents had never approved of him. But when Lindsay had started reading those motivational books by Bethany Grace, the game had changed dramatically. She'd used Bethany Grace's mantra, Happiness Is a Choice, as a response to every fight they'd had.

When Lindsay had insisted he read the then-current bestseller, *Living with Grace,* he'd done his best. He'd made it through twenty pages. The woman obviously lived in a bubble and knew nothing about actual relationships. But Lindsay thought Bethany Grace was a genius and that Happiness Is a Choice solved every issue.

Meanwhile Lindsay had consistently ignored his input regarding the business and had reminded him in many subtle ways that because she had the money, he was little more than a stable boy. It had been death by a thousand cuts. And the more angry and miserable he'd become, the more often she'd chirped that mantra: Happiness Is a Choice.

He was so lost in thought that he nearly missed the turnoff to the Triple G. The weathered sign was small and low to the ground. At the last minute he noticed it

and took the turn too fast. He sent up a rooster tail of
dust and avoided taking out the pathetic little sign by
inches. A good thing, too. His mission involved protecting property, not destroying it.

If he'd thought the Last Chance road was poorly
maintained, it was a superhighway compared to this
collection of potholes. He slowed down in an effort to
save the truck's alignment. Any teenage trespassers
who'd braved this road might be sorry when the deep
ruts did a number on their precious first car, or worse
yet, screwed up the family SUV.

Because he had to concentrate on the miserable road
in front of him, he couldn't take stock of what was causing the smoke. The stench reached him long before he
arrived on the scene. Finally he pulled into the weed-
infested clearing surrounded by a collection of dilapidated buildings that made up the Triple G Ranch. Then
he put on the brakes and stared.

In the bare dirt area that constituted the ranch's front
yard, a leather recliner was on fire. Even more curious, a
dark-haired woman dressed in heels, a short beige skirt
and a matching jacket stood watching it, butane lighter
in hand. She seemed to be the only person around, and
was most likely the citified daughter.

A red SUV was parked beside the house, a fairly safe
distance from the blazing chair unless a spark caught
the weeds on fire. If Nash were to guess, he'd say she'd
arrived in that vehicle, but he couldn't imagine her mo-
tivation for setting the chair on fire.

That had to be deliberate. And difficult. Those chairs
were usually treated with flame retardants, which explained the god-awful smell. Gasoline had probably

been involved. Sure enough, he spotted a can lying about twenty feet away from her.

She gave him a cursory glance before returning her attention to the chair. The flames had died down, leaving a blackened, smoldering mess. She seemed to have it in for the chair, but if she intended to destroy it completely, she'd have to douse it with more gasoline and relight the fire or run over it with that shiny red SUV. Both options made Nash wince.

He decided to intervene before she proceeded to do either of those things. Emmett had asked him to check things out, so he'd do that. In the process he hoped to satisfy his curiosity, because this recliner-torching was the damnedest thing he'd ever seen and he wanted to know the reason behind it.

Climbing out of the truck, he tried not to breathe too deeply. No telling what toxic crap was in that smoke. She should smother the fire for environmental reasons, if nothing else.

At the metallic sound of the truck door closing, she looked at him again. This time she held his gaze as he walked toward her. She'd seemed pulled-together and neat at first, but the closer he came, the more that impression shifted.

She'd torn the left shoulder seam of her tailored beige jacket, and the front of her white blouse and short beige skirt were smudged with dirt. Her nylons were a mass of runs and her beige heels were scuffed beyond repair.

Apparently, despite being dressed for a day at the office, she'd dragged that chair outside before going for the gasoline and the butane lighter. Judging from her streaked makeup and the way her short dark hair was plastered to her forehead and neck, the job had made her sweat. Her mascara was smeared and she looked as if she'd been crying—either from anger or because of the foul smoke. Maybe both. His eyes stung, and he'd only been here a few minutes.

He paused when he was an arm's length away from her. Her gray eyes might be pretty if they weren't so red. When faced with a situation like this, where someone was obviously upset, Nash usually tried to lighten the mood a little. "On a redecorating kick?"

She stared at him as if he'd said something terminally stupid, which of course he had, but that was the idea. She didn't seem inclined to joke around, though. Too bad.

Swiping at her eyes with the back of her free hand, she looked him up and down. "Who are you and why are you here?"

"The name's Nash Bledsoe. I work at the Last Chance, and the foreman saw smoke and asked me to investigate. He thought trespassers might be causing a problem."

"Oh." She gazed up at the smoke spiraling into the blue sky as if only now realizing that it might be noticed by others. "Sorry about that. Everything's fine. I'm not a trespasser. I own the place. Lucky me."

She probably was the daughter, then. He could have left it at that and headed back to the Last Chance, but he decided not to. The smoke was a pollutant, and he still didn't know why she'd set fire to the chair. "Look, it's obvious that you want to get rid of this piece of furniture, but your method is spewing bad stuff into the air."

"I didn't think of that." She glanced at the smoke and the blackened, shriveled leather. "I'll bet there's not a working fire extinguisher around this place, either."

"I happen to have one in my truck. I'll get it."

She hesitated, as if reluctant to accept his help.

He gave her an encouraging smile. "That's really the way to go. Once I've sprayed it with foam, we can figure out how to get it out of here and into the landfill where it belongs."

"Maybe I'll just dig a hole and bury it."

"Would take a big hole."

"That's okay. Digging it would feel good."

He looked into her bloodshot eyes and recognized the same kind of rage, grief and frustration he'd been trying to work off by mucking out stalls. He didn't have to ask her any more questions, after all. She was mad at somebody, probably the person who'd spent time in this chair. Odds were that would have been her late father.

The combination of anger and sorrow could make people do strange things, and he certainly understood that. She seemed to recognize that she'd found a kindred spirit, because some of the defiance left her expression. As her gaze mellowed, she looked really nice, even with her mascara running and her hair all sweaty.

"I'll get the extinguisher," he said. "We can go from there."

"Okay." Her voice had grown softer, too. "Thanks."

He felt a smile coming on as he hurried back to the truck. He hadn't been any woman's hero in a very long time, and he'd missed that.

After he slimed the chair, he'd see if she had a tarp. He didn't want to load that gross thing into the back of the ranch truck without one, but if he could put it on something, he could drive straight to the landfill. She didn't need to dig a hole and bury the chair. Surely there were other menial chores around this wreck of a place where she could work out her emotions.

He returned with the extinguisher. "You might want to stand back while I do this."

She backed up several steps. Considering the uneven dirt in the front yard, she navigated well on those über-high heels. She must be used to them.

"I guess you think I'm a lunatic for trying to burn this recliner," she said.

"No, actually, I don't. I know something about being so furious that you have to find a good target for your anger."

"That about sums up my little stunt, but now it seems pretty juvenile."

"Not at all. I think it had flair." He pointed the extinguisher at the recliner. Slowly circling it, he layered on the foam. At last he was satisfied. "That should do it." He glanced over and noticed her tiny smile. She had a full, prettily shaped mouth. She'd probably clean up real good. "Feeling any better?"

"I am, actually."

"Excellent." He cleared his throat. "So you're the daughter?"

She nodded.

"I thought so. But I've gone and forgotten your first name. I was a few years ahead of you in school."

"You wouldn't have remembered me, anyway. I was an awkward nerd back then. A certified late bloomer." Her smile widened a little. "I remember you, though, Nash Bledsoe. You were quite the heartthrob."

To his dismay, he felt heat rising from his collar. "I don't know about that. Anyway, is your last name still Grace, or something else, now?" If she was married, he didn't think much of a husband who'd send her off to deal with this situation by herself.

"My last name is still Grace." She gazed at him thoughtfully. "I take it you haven't heard anything about my career, then?"

"Sorry, I haven't. Emmett just said you'd become a city girl."

"Well, that's humbling. But then, I lost touch with everyone back here, and my folks weren't much for socializing, or bragging, for that matter."

"About what?"

"I'm a bestselling author. My latest book hit number one on all the lists."

His stomach clenched. But no, it couldn't be. Coincidences like this didn't happen in real life. "What do you write?"

"Motivational books. Self-help, is how most people refer to them."

His throat went dry and his heart began to pound. "You're *Bethany Grace?*" The name came out as a hoarse croak.

"So you *have* heard of me!" She looked pleased.

"Oh, yeah." He felt light-headed. "I've heard of you. Your books made my life a living hell."

2

BETHANY GASPED. SHE'D had many reactions to her books in the three years since she'd first hit the bestseller charts, but no one had ever said anything that awful. Nash wasn't kidding, either. His blue eyes had iced over and his expression had turned to granite.

She'd just been thinking what a good-looking guy he'd turned into, and a kind one, at that. She'd found herself admiring the strong line of his jaw and the sensual curve of his lower lip. Because she'd outgrown her nerdy phase, she'd felt capable of flirting a little with the likes of Nash Bledsoe, if he wasn't attached.

But instead she'd discovered that her cheerful and positive message had created such fury in him that he'd barely been able to speak her name. To know that her books had done that made her physically ill. She hadn't eaten anything since yesterday, which was probably good, because she had nothing in her rolling stomach that could come back up.

His bitter words had sucked most of the air from her lungs, too, but she finally managed to draw in enough to ask a question. "How did my books do that?"

A muscle in his jaw twitched. "I'd rather not get into it."

"Please, don't hit me with something like that and refuse to tell me why! No one's ever... I've never had anyone tell me..." She took a shaky breath. "You look as if you *hate* me."

He scrubbed a hand over his face and gazed up at the sky. "Bethany Grace." He chuckled, but the sound had no humor in it. Then he looked at her again. "My ex-wife loves your books."

From the way he said it, Bethany knew that wasn't a good thing. "Okay."

He studied her for long enough that she became very aware of how sweaty and dirty she was. And how foolish this stunt of hers must look to him, now that he knew she was the author of bestsellers such as *Living with Grace* and her current chart-topper, *Grace Personified*. She'd always been proud of her success, but given this situation, she should have kept her mouth shut. Today was the wrong time for her to be in the glare of a spotlight that would reveal her flaws.

Too late. "I suppose you're wondering if I'm a hypocrite."

"It crossed my mind. I can't figure out why a woman who tells everyone that happiness is a choice would set fire to her daddy's recliner. That doesn't seem like a particularly cheerful move, to me." He was obviously enjoying pointing that out.

She flushed. "It wasn't. I'm not proud of my reaction. It was unworthy of me to do that."

His expression underwent a subtle change, as if that admission had soaked up some of his anger. "But oh, so very human."

"You don't have to sound so smug when you say that."

This time his chuckle was a little less caustic. "Yeah, I do. Whether you know it or not, you owe me a bit of smugness."

"What happened?"

He hesitated.

"Please. Your statement will eat at me if you don't explain where it came from."

He blew out a breath. "Okay. Short version. My in-laws were convinced that I'd only married Lindsay for her money. I think they finally convinced Lindsay, too, because she developed an attitude. She made it plain that a poor boy like me was lucky to be there."

"Ouch."

"I realize now her parents started the sabotage early and gradually turned up the heat, the way you cook a frog without the frog even noticing. I became more and more irritable. Then Lindsay found your books and felt free to remind me that Happiness Is a Choice."

She was appalled. "That's *not* how my books are supposed to be read. You can't undermine someone's confidence and then berate them for not being happy enough."

"Tell that to Lindsay and her folks."

"I will if you'd like me to. I resent that they—"

"I didn't mean that literally. Don't waste your time on them. But I have to admit, seeing you in the middle of a meltdown helps. Even the sainted Bethany Grace has a bad day once in a while."

"Sainted? I never claimed to be perfect!"

"Lindsay thinks you are. As opposed to me, a person riddled with problems."

"That's ridiculous. We all have problems. I've admitted that in everything I've written." Then she had a thought. "Did *you* ever read one of my books?"

"One chapter."

She tried to remember if she'd admitted any problems in Chapter One of *Living with Grace* or the earlier books. Maybe not. "Then you stopped reading?"

"Then I threw the book against the wall."

She winced.

"Sorry, but you have to remember this was a book recommended by the woman who, with the help of her folks, was mentally torturing me. I could only take so much of the rainbows and lollipops you were handing out."

"All things considered, you probably won't ever make it through an entire book of mine, and I don't blame you. But somewhere in *Living with Grace,* maybe toward the middle, I admit to having a temper, and you've just seen me demonstrate that."

Nash glanced at the now-soggy recliner. "Pretty impressive, too. Those old recliners are heavy suckers. How long did it take you to drag it out here?"

"I don't know. I wasn't keeping track of time. I drove into the yard, walked up the rickety porch steps, went inside, saw the state of things in there and…lost it."

"You didn't know it was this bad?"

She sighed, remembering all the should-haves she'd ignored in the past year and a half. "I suspected. My parents were never savvy about the ranching business and the Triple G operated in the red quite a bit. When I started making decent money, I sent checks home." And she should have come herself. "Obviously the money wasn't used to maintain the ranch."

"Why didn't your dad get some advice from his neighbors? I'm sure anyone at the Last Chance would have been glad to—"

"Not my dad's style. He didn't like to admit he was deficient in any area. That's why he and my mom didn't mingle. He didn't feel equal to the other ranchers, so he kept to himself. Rejected any offer of help. I saw him do it several times. Eventually people stopped trying."

"That's sad."

"Incredibly sad." She glanced around her. "You see the result. After my mom died a year and a half ago, my dad started drinking a lot, apparently. Whenever I'd suggest coming home for a visit, he'd discourage me. To be honest, I wasn't eager to be here without my mom. She was always the more positive influence. And my career was heating up, so…I used that as an excuse."

"Understandable."

She appreciated that one-word comment more than he'd ever know. Nash Bledsoe *was* a kind person, just as she'd decided when he hadn't lectured her about burning the recliner. She probably didn't have to worry about him blabbing about her circumstances, but it wouldn't hurt to make sure.

She cleared her throat. "I'm not famous enough to have paparazzi following me around, but this would make a juicy story for somebody—Motivational Guru Let Father Die in Squalor. That kind of thing."

"Are you worried that I'll tell on you?"

"Not really, but after all, you have a personal grudge against me. I guess I couldn't blame you for thinking about exposing my frailties to the general public."

His blue gaze sharpened. "I'm not vindictive, Bethany."

"I didn't think so, but—"

"I'll report to Emmett that I found you here burning trash, and after we talked, you decided to take your garbage to the landfill from now on. He doesn't seem to know who you are. I'd be surprised if anyone in this area realizes that you're nationally known in the motivational field. Cowboys don't read those books all that much."

"No need. They live a blessed life." She smiled in gratitude. "Thanks, Nash."

"So what are you going to do? I mean, besides destroying this recliner?"

"I have to sell the place. My life's in Atlanta now. Keeping property in Jackson Hole makes no sense, except…"

"Except?"

"I worry about selling it as is. If the media somehow finds out my dad lived like this… But hiring somebody to fix it up is risky, too. Word could still get out."

"So hire me."

"You? You have a job."

"True, but it's only sunup to sundown. My nights are my own. My dad was a general contractor and I worked with him every summer during high school and college. And I could use the money."

She couldn't help laughing. "You can't work on repairs in the dark."

"Inside stuff I can, and for outside stuff, I can set up spotlights. It's completely doable."

"Will the folks at the Last Chance object to having you moonlight, literally?"

He shrugged. "Not if I tell them that we're old schoolmates and you're helping me financially by hiring me during my off-hours. They all know I'm saving up for my own place, and this will make perfect sense to them."

She considered his offer. Although she didn't really know him, all her instincts told her he was trustworthy. Besides, he worked for the Chances, who were known for their integrity. That was a recommendation in itself, and he'd certainly be a better bet than taking potluck with some stranger.

"There's a lot to be done here." She looked around. "It's been neglected for several years. Are you sure you can manage by yourself?"

He nodded. "One thing I'm good at is working hard and fast. That didn't mean much to Lindsay and her parents, but it's my strength."

"I'd want you to start with the outbuildings to give me a chance to clear out any personal things from the house."

"That's fine. How long are you here for?"

"A week. That should be enough time for me to sort through the stuff in the house. And I'll be available if you have questions as you get started."

"So it's a deal?"

"It's a deal. I'll pay you well for this, Nash."

He smiled. "I'm counting on it. So let's see. Are your dad's tools still here?"

"Oh, I'm sure they are. I can't guarantee the condition of anything, but you'll need to pick up some building materials, so you can replace any broken tools then." Discussing the restoration of this place gave her a boost of energy.

"Okay, good. I figure tonight I'll come over and mostly assess the situation and come up with an estimate. Maybe I'll start on whatever doesn't require new lumber and nails. I'll give you a list you can call in to the Shoshone Feed Store. They carry building supplies, too. I'll pick everything up."

"Or I could." She pointed to the SUV. "That can haul stuff."

"Nah, don't get that shiny rental all dirty. A truck's better, anyway." He glanced at the chair. "And please leave this right here. I'll deal with it tonight."

"You're sure?"

"Part of the job. But if you want to buy some pots of flowers for the porch, that might be a nice touch."

She felt a tug of nostalgia. "My mother always had flower pots there."

"Think curb appeal."

"I will." But instead she was thinking about her mother, and the good times they'd had planting bright annuals every spring—mostly pansies and petunias. She'd forgotten that. And after the flowers had started blooming, she and her mom would sit on the porch with glasses of lemonade and admire their efforts.

She swallowed a lump of sorrow and sniffed away her tears. She grieved her dad, though she'd emotionally distanced herself from him years ago. Her mom's death still tugged at her heartstrings. But she'd rather not let that show and appear even more vulnerable. A girl had to preserve her pride.

"So if you'll get the spotlights today, I'll be here after dinner," Nash said.

"It's a deal." For the first time since she'd received the news of her father's death last week, she felt hopeful that she would be able to handle this painful inheritance.

"And don't touch that recliner."

Looking at it, she reached deep and found the humor

buried in the situation. She grinned at Nash. "I promise not to touch it. I think I've created enough recliner chaos. But hey, it brought you over here."

"And against all odds, that turns out to be a good thing."

"Yes." She met his gaze. "Yes, it does." To her great surprise, she felt a sexual tug as she looked into his blue eyes. Whoops. Better not go there. Earlier she'd considered flirting with him to prove to herself that she'd outgrown her gawky phase, but that would have been ill-advised, too.

Coming back here and facing her dad's death, and actually, her mom's as well, had stirred up some deep feelings. What seemed like sexual desire might be simply a need to be held by a big, strong cowboy. She'd had that fantasy as a teenager but thought she'd outgrown it after leaving Jackson Hole.

Judging from her reaction to Nash, she still harbored that fantasy. If he was going to be around every night for the next week, she might want to dial back that flare of desire she was feeling. She didn't need to complicate her life.

"See you tonight, Bethany." He touched the brim of his hat in a typical cowboy gesture and walked back to his truck, carrying the fire extinguisher.

God help her, she watched him leave. He had the denim-encased buns and the loose-hipped stride that turned the simple act of walking into an art form. He'd been a good-looking kid in high school who'd grown into a gorgeous man.

Her reaction might also have to do with her recent period of unintended celibacy. When *Living with Grace* hit the number one spot on several charts, she'd been swept up in a whirlwind of publicity. The media attention, plus her deadline for the next book, had caused her to abandon everything not related to her blossoming career. She hadn't been seriously involved with a man at the time, so her sex life had been easy to set aside, too.

She hadn't missed it at all, or so she'd thought until she watched Nash Bledsoe return to his truck. Apparently all the man had to do to get her thinking about bedroom games was give her a view of his jeans-clad backside. Inappropriate scenarios flashed before her eyes in living color.

"Nash?" His name was out of her mouth before she could stop herself.

He turned. "Yeah?"

"I, uh, bought some groceries before driving over here. If you'd like to have a quick dinner before you start working, I could provide that."

"Sure." His teeth were very white against his tanned skin. "That would be great. What time?"

"Around six?"

"I'll be here."

"See you then." She forced herself to turn and start back to the house instead of standing there like an idiot while he drove away. As she walked over the uneven ground, she admitted to herself that inviting him to dinner sent the exact wrong message. Their arrangement was about business, not social interaction.

She might be longing for some combination of emotional comfort and sexual excitement, but finding those things in Nash Bledsoe's arms would be a huge mistake. She didn't believe in temporary affairs, and she had the career move of a lifetime waiting for her in Atlanta on

Opal!, the most popular talk show on television, starring fan favorite Opal Knightly.

Bethany had been an occasional guest, and a friendship had formed. Now she was about to become a permanent feature on the program. Opal had mentored others by giving them a regular segment, and if ratings were good enough, Bethany might eventually launch her own show.

By the time she'd reminded herself of the stakes involved, she'd made it to the porch and Nash's truck could be heard slowly navigating the washboard road back to the highway. She decided to record her long-term goal—to have her own television show—in the day planner on her smartphone to remind herself of it daily. But first she needed a change of clothes at the least, and maybe a shower.

She chose her old bathroom instead of the master because hers was far cleaner. It obviously hadn't been used since she'd been here for her mom's funeral eighteen months ago. But when she saw her reflection in the medicine-cabinet mirror, she was appalled.

The woman in the mirror, who looked like she belonged in a low-budget horror flick, was none other than Bethany Grace, Ph.D. This was the face Nash Bledsoe had seen when he arrived. Wearing this face, with its mascara-ringed, bloodshot eyes, shiny nose and dirt-smudged cheeks, she'd considered flirting with him because now she was past her gawky stage. *Not.*

She'd looked like this, with her torn jacket and filthy blouse, when she'd struck a deal for his handyman services and then casually, or not so casually, invited him to dine with her. And the crazy man had said *yes.* He must really need the money.

As she imagined what he'd been thinking all through their exchange, she started to laugh. The more she thought about it, the harder she laughed, until she had to lean against the vanity for support. If her adoring public could only see her now. Fortunately, they couldn't, and Nash wouldn't tell on her.

In a way, it was a relief that he'd seen her at her worst. Probably a relief for him, too, after the image he'd grown to hate during the months when his ex had battered him with Bethany's perky little message, Happiness Is a Choice.

Funny thing, though. Bethany believed that message. Her father had been an insecure man who didn't know how to be happy and her mother had tried her best to keep a pleasant home while married to someone who lacked the confidence to live life to the fullest. Bethany had studied psychology until she'd finally understood all that and was able to create a different pattern.

The cornerstone of that new pattern was that circumstances couldn't always be changed, but attitudes could. Her father had chosen to be unhappy. Her mother, for the most part, had chosen to be happy. Had she been a stronger person, she might have also chosen to leave. Part of Bethany's grief over her mom's death was regret that her mother hadn't enjoyed a better marriage.

Bethany had written her books as much for herself as for others. They'd struck a chord with the public, and while she'd received a few slightly negative reviews, most of the feedback had been positive. Nash had handed her the most devastating critique yet.

He'd demonstrated how her words could be twisted and used against someone in crisis. At least that would make her a better writer, and now that she was about to launch her new venture, a better talk show personality.

Being linked with Opal meant Bethany had to be careful not to embarrass her fairy godmother. Opal knew all about the situation in Jackson Hole, and she'd cautioned Bethany to keep it under wraps. Bethany intended to do exactly that.

At some point she might tell Nash about her new opportunity so he could better understand the stakes involved. Ah, Nash. Inevitably her thoughts returned to the bodacious Mr. Bledsoe.

He'd had a Reputation with a capital *R* back in high school. Nash had hung around with Jack Chance back then, and another buddy, Langford "Hutch" Hutchinson. The three of them had cut quite a swath through the senior-class girls.

If Nash had been good at making love when he was eighteen, and he'd had years to practice his technique since then…it didn't have anything to do with her, right?

With a sigh of longing that would go unsatisfied, she glanced at the small battery-operated clock on the counter. It was pink, like everything in this bathroom, a holdover from when she'd chosen the color scheme at fourteen. Amazingly, the batteries had lasted since she'd replaced them a year and a half ago. The clock told her that she had many hours before Nash would show up for dinner.

She had time to drive into Shoshone and get those spotlights he needed. But first she'd shower, change clothes, choose a menu for tonight and figure out how to make the dining room a more welcoming place. She might never erase his first impression of her as a chair-burning maniac with smeared makeup and ruined clothes, but she could mute that impression.

After all, she was the author of *Living with Grace,* and she knew how to create a lovely dining experience. Maybe she shouldn't have invited Nash to dinner, but now that she had, she'd damned well do it right.

3

NASH WAS GLAD FOR AN excuse to leave the Last Chance when five-thirty rolled around. All eight boys in the Last Chance Youth Program had arrived. They ranged in age from twelve to fourteen, and they were all hyper. Emmett had assured Nash they'd settle down once they were put to work, but that wouldn't happen until tomorrow. Tonight they were like Mexican jumping beans. Very loud Mexican jumping beans.

Pete, Sarah's fiancé and the philanthropist who'd dreamed up the concept, had divided the boys into teams for a relay race in the yard before dinner. He'd roped Nash's buddy Luke Griffin into helping. Luke had the kind of easygoing attitude that made him perfect for the job.

Nash didn't know much about kids, so he left with a wave and a smile. He admired Pete's humanitarianism and was thrilled that Sarah had found someone worthy of her. Jonathan Chance would have been a tough act to follow, but Pete seemed to be up to the challenge.

Nash took his own truck for the drive to the Triple G. He couldn't justify wearing out the shocks on a Last

Chance truck for a side job. Besides that, he intended to haul away what was left of the recliner when he left tonight, and if he used his pickup, he wouldn't have to worry about the mess.

Deciding what to wear for this first night of work had been a chore. He expected to get dirty when he tackled the repairs, but she'd invited him to dinner, so he didn't want to show up in ratty clothes for that. In reality, he wanted to look good no matter whether he was eating at her table or working on her outbuildings.

That was stupid of him, but he couldn't seem to help himself. She remembered him as a high school stud, and he didn't want to destroy that memory by dressing like a hobo. So he'd compromised on middle-of-the-road jeans, shirt, hat and boots. They were nicer than he'd wear to muck out stalls, but not new enough for a Saturday night trip to the Spirits and Spurs.

All of it would wash except the boots and hat. He could take the hat off because the sun would be going down, and the boots usually cleaned up pretty well with some saddle soap. He'd also showered and shaved before changing into those clothes, which he'd caught some guff from Luke about. He'd wanted to know why Nash was getting spit-shined before going off to do carpentry.

Nash had told Sarah and Jack that he would be working for the Graces' daughter, but he hadn't gone into detail about her. He had to be especially careful when mentioning the job to Luke, who might recognize Bethany Grace's name. Everyone at the stable in Sacramento had heard about her books from Lindsay.

But Luke was more interested in the possibility that Nash might finally be coming out of retirement. His shower and shave had given Luke the idea that romance was brewing. No matter how many times Nash had denied it, Luke had continued to tease him about being her *handy*man.

The teasing had hit home, whether Luke knew it or not. Right before he'd left Bethany's this morning, they'd had a moment. A silent exchange had taken place, one that any man or woman with a pulse understood.

He didn't plan to act on it, and he doubted that she wanted him to. She was focused on the next stage in her career. Besides, she was paying him to do an honest night's work, and adding mattress bingo into the deal skated a little too close to sex for hire.

Plus, if he needed more reasons to curb any lust he felt toward her, he'd remind himself that she lost her dad a week ago. And besides, she had money and he did not. He knew how that sort of situation played out, and only a fool jumped into the same kettle of hot water twice. She needed him to help her make the Triple G attractive to buyers. End of story.

This time he didn't miss the turnoff to her ranch, but a day of baking in the June sun hadn't improved the road any. It was while he slowly maneuvered around the potholes and deep ruts that inspiration struck. Once the idea came to him, he couldn't imagine why he hadn't thought of it sooner. The solution to her problem and his was obvious. He would buy the ranch from her.

Sure, it would take some creative financing and wipe out the savings he'd carefully accumulated so far. But there were programs for first-time buyers, something he'd researched not long ago. Lindsay's parents had given them a house as a wedding present, and so that meant he was, in fact, a first timer.

What a brainstorm! The ranch abutted the Last Chance,

so he could keep in close touch with his friends. It was small, but that made it more likely he could swing the deal. He might not even want more land than this. And the view of the Tetons was almost as spectacular as the Last Chance had.

If she went for this solution and still wanted him to do repairs, he'd consider it sweat equity instead of taking money for it. She wouldn't be ready to turn the property over to him until she'd finished her sorting inside the house, but she could forget the hassle of listing the place and considering offers, so he'd actually save her time in the long run.

He also had a hunch she wasn't selling the ranch for the money. Maybe selling to someone she knew, someone who loved this area and would make the ranch into a showplace, would compensate for his lack of a sizable chunk of cash. He was so eager to broach the plan that he sped up and hit a rut that nearly jolted the eyeballs out of his skull.

Forcing himself back to a crawl, he allowed himself to dream of actually owning this ranch. Because he wouldn't have income from it right away, he'd keep his job at the Last Chance. He'd sink every penny into improvements, and eventually buy a couple of horses. And he'd get a dog.

Maybe he'd turn it into a boarding stable. He understood how to run one of those, thanks to Lindsay. She'd had the business degree and he'd had the animal science degree. On paper it had seemed like the perfect match. Luke had reported that horse-care standards at the stable had fallen quickly after Nash had left.

The drive to the Triple G, which he'd already started thinking of as his, took freaking forever. He had time to decide what color he'd paint the barn—deep red—and whether he needed shutters on the ranch house windows. Probably not. He hoped that at least one of the corrals was solid, because he desperately wanted a couple of horses. Without horses, what kind of ranch was it, anyway?

When he finally pulled into the clearing, he saw that the recliner remained in the middle of the yard like an abstract chunk of modern art. At least it didn't smell quite so bad now. Next he noticed four colored pots—red, yellow, blue and green—lined up on the front porch. Each was filled with an array of petunias, daisies and pansies.

He'd keep those pots and refill them every spring. It was amazing how flowers in pots classed up a place. Even the weathered gray boards on the porch looked better because of those flowers, almost as if the weathering had been left that way on purpose, for artistic effect.

After parking his truck next to her rented SUV, he started toward the front porch steps. She must have heard the engine, because she opened the screen door and came out. He almost didn't recognize her.

This morning he'd thought she might clean up pretty good and be reasonably attractive. Time to reevaluate. She'd shot way past attractive and traveled straight on to beautiful.

Her glossy cap of dark hair curled around her ears and made him want to slide his fingers into that black silk to see if it felt as good as it looked. She probably had on makeup, but she was skilled enough for it to be invisible. That left her with a wholesome and very kissable face, big gray eyes and a sweetly rounded chin that begged to be cupped in one hand while he combed through her hair with the other. He could almost taste her lips.

She'd traded in the damaged suit for a ruffled white sleeveless blouse and gray capris. She wore sandals that showed off lavender toenails. He could eat her up with a spoon. But he'd thought of a great idea while he was driving here, and he should tell her what it was…just as soon as he remembered. Seeing her looking so sexy and approachable had made him forget everything else.

"You're right on time." She smiled, which warmed him in a way he hadn't been warmed in a very long while.

"I was eager to leave." Although his brain wasn't working very well, his gift of gab seemed functional. "I don't know if you've heard about the Last Chance Youth Program. It just started, and the place is overrun with wild adolescent boys."

She shook her head. "I hadn't heard, but what a cool idea. You don't like kids?"

"Sure, in small numbers. Eight of them running around the ranch is…a lot."

"They'll be living there?"

"Until the middle of August. The idea is to take boys from troubled situations and give them a couple months of ranch life. With luck they'll leave with a work ethic and maybe even some self-esteem."

"I love it. If I were staying, I'd want to see if I could help."

Nash grimaced. "Which makes me the guy with the bad attitude who's griping about the mayhem involved."

"Not at all. Not everybody's in love with kids that age. You have a right not to be."

He thought about that. "No, I don't. I'm at the Last Chance because the folks there believe in giving both people and animals one more shot at success. That's what this program is about, too, and I'm going to adjust my thinking."

Taking a deep breath, he smiled at her. He'd love to compliment her on how nice she looked, but that might not be appropriate for the hired hand. "The flower pots sure spruce up the porch."

"Thanks!" She seemed genuinely pleased. "I thought so, too. Hungry?"

Now there was a loaded question. "Sure am. Something smells really good." He actually meant her, because she gave off a delicate scent that reminded him of plants that flowered only in moonlight. He'd learned about those while he'd lived in California.

But she'd think he was referring to the smell of food coming from the kitchen, and that was fine. They should keep their interaction platonic, or as close to platonic as they could manage given that they were both healthy and human. Looking at her in the soft light of early evening, he was feeling very human, indeed.

"It's chicken," she said. "Not very exciting, I'm afraid. Come on in."

He followed close enough that he could hold the screen door for her and breathe in her night-blooming flower scent. "I don't cook, so anything more than peanut butter and jelly is exciting to me." He might be wise to stop talking about what excited him, since Bethany had chicken beat by a country mile.

"Don't look at the living room," she said as she walked quickly through it. "I haven't had time to do much in here."

"I bunk with a bunch of cowhands. You can't shock me." But he tried to honor her request and not notice that the room was shabby and unkempt. No liquor bottles were lying around, but the faint smell of whiskey lingered. Once you spilled liquor on carpet, the stink was hard to get out. Maybe she hadn't needed much gasoline to light that recliner on fire, after all. He understood her fierce desire to haul it out of here.

The living room was separated from the dining room by French doors, and when she opened them, he walked from a miserable space into a joyous one. "Wow. You've been working hard."

"You have no idea how I loved making at least one room in this house look the way it's supposed to."

He surveyed the flickering candles on the table and the sideboard, the flowered centerpiece, the white linen tablecloth and what had to be her mother's best china, silverware and stemmed glasses. A modest crystal chandelier above the table sparkled and as the sun drifted lower in the sky, its rays shone through clean windows. He'd bet she'd washed the curtains, too.

"I can tell." He gazed at her, touched by all the effort she'd made. "I'm honored to be your guest."

She flushed. "I did it as much for me as for you. I wouldn't want you to think that I was trying to…to create a romantic setting for some reason."

"No, no, I'm sure you weren't." Damn. He hadn't thought of that, but it would have been kind of nice if she had.

"I mean, for all I know you have a girlfriend, and I—"

"No girlfriend, but you're headed off to Atlanta, where you may have a boyfriend."

"No boyfriend, but I am headed off to Atlanta." She gestured toward the festive table. "This was just a whim, to make the house seem a little bit happy again."

"Right. I completely get that." No boyfriend, but she wasn't interested in pursuing anything with him. Okay. He should be relieved, because they had no business getting involved, but from the minute she'd stepped out on that porch, he'd found himself wishing that somehow they could…what?

He'd already had this talk with himself. It went against his moral code to get cozy with the woman who was paying him to make some quick repairs so she could sell the place. And that was when he finally remembered the idea he'd had driving in here.

Once he remembered, he had trouble not blurting it out, but that wouldn't be the best way to approach such an important discussion. He should lead up to the topic. She had wineglasses on the table. Although he was opposed to drinking on the job, maybe tonight he should make an exception, because this idea might go better if it was presented over a glass of wine.

If she accepted his offer to buy the house, would that change the dynamic between them? Then he'd be a buyer, not an employee. His moral code might allow him to get cozy with the seller of the property he was purchasing. After all, why not? Because she might think that was a really bad plan, that was why not.

"Nash? Are you okay?"

He blinked and wondered how long he'd been standing there staring into space as if he had buckshot for brains. "I'm fine. Sorry. Got lost in thought for a minute."

"I noticed. You looked a bit startled, and I hope this setting didn't trigger a bad memory."

"It's not that at all."

"Are you sure? Because I can blow out the candles and we can eat out on the front porch. It takes time to get over a divorce. Sometimes a situation will blindside you with memories, good or bad."

"You've been divorced?"

"No, but I talked to plenty of divorced people back when I was working full-time as a counselor. I can tell it was a painful event. So if all this reminds you of something to do with your ex, then let's—"

"Not at all. This is great."

She took a deep breath. "I'm glad you like it. I put out the wineglasses automatically, but we don't have to drink wine. You may not want to, considering that you'll be working later."

"Let's have a glass of wine," Nash said. "I'm a big guy, so one glass won't put me under the table. And we should toast getting one room looking really good." There, he'd finally managed to get them on a safe track.

She smiled. "That would be lovely. Stay right there. I'll be back in a flash with the wine and the food."

"I'll help." He started to follow her into the kitchen.

"No." She turned so abruptly that he bumped into her.

Although she backed away immediately, his body still felt the imprint of hers—soft, yielding, delicious. He closed his hands into fists so he wouldn't do something really stupid and reach for her.

She'd been affected by the accidental contact, too. Her pupils widened with awareness. She might be head-

ing off to Atlanta, but that didn't stop her from being
attracted to him. That was gratifying.

She cleared her throat. "I don't want you to come
into the kitchen. I scrubbed it down, but it still isn't
very pretty. The dining room is, and I want to maintain the illusion."

"Having you wait on me doesn't seem right."

"Humor me, okay?"

He relented, partly because she looked so incredibly
beautiful standing there with the light from the chandelier sparkling in her eyes. He also realized that she'd
encountered mostly ugliness when she'd walked into the
house earlier today. If limiting his view to this dining
room helped her cope, then he'd go along.

"All right," he said. "But I refuse to sit down like
some lord of the manor. I'll stay standing until I can
help you into your chair."

She nodded. "It's a good compromise." With that she
turned and walked over to the pocket door leading into
the kitchen. "No peeking. Enjoy the sunset."

Because he wanted to make her happy, he walked
over to the set of two double-hung windows that faced
southwest and watched an orange sun slide behind a
bank of clouds. From here he could see a little bit of
the Grand Tetons to his right. The house wasn't angled
to capitalize on a view of the majestic range. The best
spot might be at the back, and he wondered if there was
a porch out there.

If not, he'd add one. Ah, listen to him, talking in his
head as if she'd already agreed to sell him the Triple G.
But he couldn't think why she wouldn't.

Then a very logical reason came to him. Obviously
making this dining room pretty again had been a labor

of love. The crystal chandelier told him that at one time, someone, probably her mother, had tried to bring cheer into this house.

Now Bethany was attempting to do the same thing by rescuing the house, room by room. As she gradually removed the ugliness her father had created and replaced it with beauty, she might begin to love her old family home again. In the meantime Nash would improve the look of the outbuildings so they wouldn't be depressing anymore, either.

Sure, Atlanta was a long way from Wyoming, but her decision to sell might be a knee-jerk reaction to her father's neglect of the place followed by his undignified death. Once the house and outbuildings looked decent, though, she might decide to keep the ranch.

He still planned to ask if she'd sell it to him, but his conscience would require him to add that she could change her mind later. That was the right thing to do. But as he contemplated how this could turn out, his cherished dream began to crumble.

4

BETHANY HAD WONDERED if she and Nash would have anything to say to each other over dinner. Just because he was built like a Greek god didn't mean that he could carry on a conversation. Turned out he was excellent at it. She couldn't remember the last time she'd laughed so much during a meal.

They sat kitty-corner from each other at the large oval table. She'd arranged the place settings that way because it had seemed friendlier, and from the easy way they'd talked to each other during the meal, anyone might think they were old friends.

They reminisced about Jackson High School and teachers they'd had. They shared a lot of the same opinions about who had been great and who should have been fired. She discovered that Nash had a degree in animal science and they had a lively debate on the differences between animal psychology and people psychology.

"If animals could talk, we could settle this once and for all," Bethany said. She took a sip of her wine and wondered why there was still so much left in her glass.

"Thank God they can't!" Nash leaned back in his chair and picked up his glass, which was as full as hers. His plate was empty, though. "I lost my virginity in a barn. I'm sure the stallions would have razzed me about my technique if they'd been able to comment during the event. Plus I'd snuck out there with the school superintendent's daughter, and naturally I didn't want that information spread around. I could have been expelled."

Picturing Nash having sex, even virginal sex, was having a predictable effect on her. She hoped he'd attribute her flush to the wine. She glanced at the bottle and discovered that it was empty. It dawned on her that Nash must have refilled their glasses at some point and she'd been having too much fun to notice.

"I hadn't thought of animals being tattletales," she said. "I guess it's a good thing they can't talk. I lost my virginity to my then-boyfriend when his parents weren't home, and as I remember, there was a cat lying on his desk. She probably saw the whole thing."

"Kinky." He grinned at her. "Are you one of those women who likes having an audience?"

"No, I most certainly do not! It was a *cat,* not a person. And frankly, it sort of freaked me out when I noticed her staring at us." She took another swallow of wine and realized she was feeling extremely mellow. And all this talk of sex was turning her on. "Do *you* like an audience?" If he did, that would help cool her off. She wasn't into that.

Of course, she wasn't supposed to be feeling hot in the first place. And she'd never bothered to record her long-term goal in her day planner, either. The double whammy of wine and sexy conversation made her wonder why boinking Nash would interfere with having her own television show someday. The extremely boinkable Nash Bledsoe was looking yummier by the minute.

"I prefer privacy when I'm making love to a woman." His voice had lowered to a sexy drawl and his blue gaze held hers. "I don't like the idea of being interrupted."

Oh, Lordy. She could hardly breathe from wanting him. "Me, either."

He put down his glass and leaned toward her. "I have a confession to make."

"Me, too."

"Okay, you first, then."

She took another hefty swallow of wine, for courage. "You know when I claimed that this nice dinner wasn't supposed to be romantic?"

"Yeah."

"I lied."

"Oh, really?" His blue eyes darkened to navy. "Care to elaborate?"

"See, you were this out-of-reach senior back in high school, and I was a nerdy freshman, so when you showed up today, I thought about flirting with you because now I actually have the confidence to do that. But then you offered to help repair the place, so I *couldn't* flirt with you. But I still thought you were really hot. We shouldn't have sex, though. At least, I didn't think so this morning, but then I fixed up the dining room, and I admit you were on my mind while I did that. So I think secretly I wanted it to be romantic. But I—"

"Do you always talk this much after two glasses of wine?" He'd moved even closer, bare inches away.

She could smell his shaving lotion. Then she realized what that meant. He'd shaved before coming over here. That was significant. "I didn't have two full glasses."

"I think you did."

She glanced at her wineglass, which was now empty. Apparently she'd been babbling and drinking at the same time. "You poured me a second glass." When he started to respond, she stopped him. "But that's okay, because if you hadn't, I wouldn't be admitting to you that I want you so much that I almost can't stand it, and you wouldn't be looking at me as if you actually might be considering the idea of…"

"Of what?" He was within kissing distance.

"This." She grabbed his face in both hands and planted one on that smiling mouth of his. And oh, it was glorious. Nash Bledsoe had the best mouth of any man she'd ever kissed. Once she'd made the initial contact, he took over, and before she quite realized it, he'd pulled her out of her chair and was drawing her away from the table.

"Bedroom," he murmured between kisses. "Where is it?"

She thought fast, or as fast as the wine would allow. "Follow me." She eased out of his arms and took his hand. "And don't look at anything."

"You're all that I see."

Ah, he was good, this guy. He knew his lines, and she had a feeling he'd know the right moves, too. Shoving open the pocket door, she led him through the kitchen. Fortunately she'd turned out the light so it was dim in there.

Her bedroom and bath were off the kitchen. She only had a twin bed, and the room's color scheme was as pink as the bathroom and included ruffles. She didn't think he'd care, though, especially if she didn't turn on the light and he wasn't faced with all the girlie frills from the get-go. "Don't worry," she said. "I have condoms."

"You do?" He sounded amused. "Since when?"

"Since I went shopping today. And I told myself I wasn't going to have sex with you, but then I thought, *What if he seduces me but forgot the condoms?*"

"Good thought."

"I like covering my options." Once they were inside her bedroom, she turned and moved into his arms. "*Were* you going to seduce me?"

"No. Or I would have brought condoms." He cupped her chin and turned her face up to his. "But I'm perfectly willing to be seduced."

"Oh, good." With a sigh, she nestled against him. "Except I'm not so good at seduction. Not a lot of practice."

He laughed. "Then I'll take it from here."

"Sure. That would be great." Once he started kissing her again, she knew she'd made the right decision. This cowboy knew his way around a seduction. She was in the hands of a master.

And what hands they were, too—large and strong, hands that could gentle a horse or excite a woman with equal skill. Because she'd bolted straight to city life after high school, she'd never been loved by a man who worked with his hands. Serious omission on her part.

With the kind of dexterity that could repair a broken bridle or braid a rope, he unfastened the buttons down the front of her sleeveless blouse. And he did it while kissing the living daylights out of her. His tongue did things to her mouth that, if employed elsewhere on her body, would be illegal in some states. She hoped he was into breaking a law or two.

The man also knew how to get a woman out of her bra, and once he did, he demonstrated how much he understood the sensitivity of breasts in general and nipples in particular. Oh, dear God. She trembled on the edge of an orgasm, and he'd only stroked her breasts.

He lifted his mouth from hers. "You feel incredible."

"You, too."

Laughter rippled through his response. "You haven't touched me yet."

Oh. She'd meant that his hands on her breasts felt incredible, but in her dazed state of pure pleasure, she'd abandoned her side of the deal. "Sorry."

His breath was warm as he nuzzled the spot behind her ear. "You don't have a thing to be sorry about. You invited me into your bedroom and you have condoms. But I'd appreciate it if you'd unzip my jeans."

"Glad to." She eased back and slid her hand down to reach for his zipper, where she discovered that the denim covering his crotch was stretched to the breaking point. Tugging down his zipper wouldn't be easy, but once she did, she was in for a treat.

She found the zipper tab, but the physics of the situation worked against her. She made no progress whatsoever.

"Unfasten my belt buckle and the top snap, first."

She was amazed that he could even talk, considering the fact that he'd already unbuttoned and unzipped her capris and was presently working them down over her hips. That was enough to make her speechless, but not him, apparently. She turned her attention to his belt buckle.

When she got it undone and managed to unhook the metal button, too, his breath caught. She drew the metal zipper down and he quivered. Until that point, she'd thought the power was all on his side, but not so.

She shoved his briefs down along with his jeans, and he gasped.

Or maybe she'd sucked in a breath. Didn't matter. She had a grip on him now, and once she'd wrapped her hands around the amazing length and breadth of what had been constrained inside those briefs, she was awed…and grateful. If not for a burning recliner and a bottle of wine later on, she might never have held such a treasure, or anticipated the joy that treasure might bring.

She started to sink to her knees.

"No, wait." He grasped her by her elbows and drew her back up. "Let's get rid of the rest of our clothes. Once you start doing that, I won't want to stop for anything, and I can't maneuver when we're still dressed."

"You bet." While he pulled off his boots, she nudged off her sandals and stepped out of her panties and capris. The soft light of the sunset filtered through her pink sheer curtains and gave the room a rosy glow. She'd never brought a man, or even a teenage boy, here before. She was glad the place held no memories of other guys. That made tonight unique.

"There." Tossing the last of his things to the floor, he stood before her in all his aroused glory. The evening shadows made him seem slightly mysterious, a phantom man come to claim her. "Where were we?"

In the semidarkness, she grew bold. "I think we left off here." She flattened her palms against his sculpted chest. Leaning forward, she pressed her mouth against his breastbone. His skin was hot, and his heart throbbed against her hand.

He tasted like heaven and sin all wrapped up in the musky aroma of pure male. Slowly she made her way down his torso, hands stroking, mouth nibbling, until she reached her goal and dropped to her knees. As she curled her fingers around his generous endowment, he groaned.

"I thought you weren't any good at this." He sounded hoarse and not nearly as in control as he had been moments ago.

"I'm not." She placed a soft kiss on the head of his penis.

He sucked in a breath. "I beg to differ."

"Maybe you inspire me." He might never realize how much. Obviously she'd never abandoned the fantasy of a cowboy lover—strong and daring, yet tender and kind—but she'd never indulged that fantasy. Tonight she would.

His voice was strained. "Bethany…"

"I'm here." With that, she took him into her mouth and felt the power of making a man her slave.

Nash gripped her head with both hands and his big body shook. She was no expert at this, but a girl only had to use her imagination. She already knew that this significant body part was extremely sensitive, and she assumed that the swirl of her tongue and the suction of her mouth would register high on his personal Richter scale.

That assumption proved true. As she paid exceptionally close attention to his penis, his breathing changed dramatically. Soft moans turned into gasps and heartfelt groans of approval.

Even better, his excitement fueled hers. She was really getting into the project when he pressed his fingertips into her scalp. "Stop."

Temporarily pulling back, she gazed up at him. "Something wrong, cowboy?" She'd always wanted to address a man as *cowboy,* and now she had the real deal right in front of her.

"I…" He cleared his throat. "I'm too close."

"Need a breather?"

"No." He gulped in air. "I need…a condom. Please."

She could read between the lines. He was a considerate lover who wanted to make sure he took care of his lady before he came. Chalk up one more point for Nash Bledsoe.

"I'll get the box." She rose to her feet and discovered she was pretty darned shaky, too.

"Hurry."

"They're in the bathroom." She went into her attached bath accompanied by the sound of pillows hitting the floor and linens being yanked back with a decisive swoosh. He was obviously making good use of his time to prepare the bed for sex.

She grabbed the box from under the counter and turned to find him right there, hand out.

"I'll open it." His voice was low and urgent as he stepped aside. "Go lie down."

If she hadn't been half crazed with lust, she would have laughed at his abrupt command. But light from the setting sun revealed the lines of strain on his face. He was holding back with great effort, and losing control would break his personal code of sexual conduct.

He ripped open the cardboard box. "Sorry. *Please* go lie down."

"Glad to." Walking into her bedroom, she noticed that her twin bed had been stripped down to the bottom sheet. Her comforter and all the pillows, both the practical and decorative ones, had been tossed to the floor.

Nash seemed to be ready for streamlined action, and

she was only too happy to oblige. Good thing she'd packed away her stuffed animals the last time she'd been home. How embarrassing if he'd had to move teddy bears to clear the way for wild jungle sex.

As per his terse instructions, she stretched out on the pink sheet, although it didn't seem so pink in this light. The sheet had been softened by many launderings. Years ago she used to lie on this bed and imagine that someone like Nash, sometimes even Nash himself, was about to ravish her. Her heart pounded with anticipation. Fiction was about to become fact.

Tearing open a foil packet and muttering a curse under his breath, he strode back into the room. "I'm not usually like this."

"Naked?"

"Desperate." He glanced up as he approached the bed. As his gaze focused on her, he stopped in his tracks. "Good God, Bethany. You're magnificent."

The dim light hid her flush, and she was glad for that, because she wanted to seem at least a little bit sophisticated. "I wouldn't say I'm—"

"I'm the guy looking at you, and I say you are magnificent." He tossed the half-open condom packet on the nightstand. "And I'd be a fool to rush this."

"Maybe I want you to." As she surveyed his impressive package, she ached with a fierceness that made her suck in a breath. "You're pretty magnificent yourself."

"I'm standard-issue." He put a knee on the bed and braced a hand on either side of her shoulders. "You, however, are a masterpiece and deserve to be treated accordingly." His massive chest heaved. "Instead of being assaulted by some lust-crazed maniac."

His penis jutted proudly, and she couldn't resist

reaching for it. "Being assaulted by you has a certain appeal."

He circled her wrist with strong fingers. "Not the first time. Let go of me, Bethany."

"Why should I?" She rather liked having a handle on him, so to speak.

"Because now that I see you stretched out on this bed, I have a plan."

Her heartbeat thundered in her ears. "Which is?"

"To turn you inside out."

Now there was a showstopper of a promise. She had trouble dragging in enough air to ask the question. "How?"

"If you let go of me, you'll find out. If you keep squeezing me like that, you'll never know, because I'm seconds away from coming."

She released him. What woman, given those choices, wouldn't? Even in the fading light, his eyes glittered with purpose, and she wanted to find out how Nash Bledsoe approached the task of turning a woman inside out. "This bed's kind of small."

"It's big enough for my purposes. But if you need more room to flail around as I make you come, then we can move to the floor."

"I don't flail."

His smile was slow and filled with masculine confidence. "We'll see about that."

She'd never understood the concept of swooning over a guy. Gazing up at Nash she finally got it. He was the first swoon-worthy man she'd ever had sex with, and the concept made perfect sense to her now.

She would enjoy the hell out of having him in her

bed. She moistened her dry lips. "Challenge accepted. Bring it."

"Oh, I intend to, Bethany. I intend to."

5

As Nash uttered those words, which were either brave or foolish depending on how this episode ended, he hoped that he'd be able to cool himself off a little. Somehow he had to hold back the climax that had threatened to overwhelm him ever since her mouth had made contact with his cock.

She was better at this than she knew, and she'd turned him into a wild man. But the picture she'd made stretched out on the bed had brought him up short and challenged him to slow down and savor the moment. A lush body such as hers didn't show up all that often, and he was a man who'd always taken his time.

He could do that again. Moving over her, he kept their bodies from touching, except for his lips against her skin. He began with her temples. "Close your eyes." When she did, he feathered a kiss over each eyelid. "Now lie still, or as still as you can."

Her answering sigh was a quivering, tension-filled sound. He used his tongue to outline her mouth and she sighed again. "Relax," he murmured. "You're strung tight as a bow."

Her eyes opened again, and they gleamed in the twilight. "I can't relax." Her voice was low and throaty. "I want you too much."

"I'll take that as a compliment." He kept his tone light, but lust slammed into him. He tamped it down. He'd made a boast that he would turn her inside out. That would take more than a three-minute bout of frantically plunging into her.

Yet that was exactly what his body was craving. Ignoring the ache in his groin, he lowered his mouth to the pulse in her throat and nipped her there. She moaned, igniting another flare of heat in his veins. God, how he wanted to pound into her.

He'd blame abstinence for that. His divorce had left his ego battered, and he'd made a conscious decision to wait a while before getting involved with someone new. How ironic that he was breaking his sexual fast with Bethany Grace.

And yet, how fitting, too. Her books, intentionally or not, had affected his self-confidence. Providing her with mind-blowing orgasms would do a lot to restore his faith in himself. He hadn't planned for the evening to go this way, but if she wanted to lead him to temptation, he'd make her damned glad she had.

Yes, driving Bethany Grace slowly insane was far more important than satisfying his urgent need to have her. She'd primly informed him that she didn't flail. There would be some justice in being the guy who made her come completely undone.

That goal helped him focus. Pushing aside his own need for release, he began a leisurely journey over her hot, silky skin. He paid special attention to her full breasts and her nipples as they puckered beneath his tongue.

When she arched her back with a whimper of need, he applied gentle suction. He loved both the sensation of tugging on her nipple and her little gasp of pleasure. His cock loved those things, too, and it throbbed with impatience. The condom waited on the bedside table, taunting him.

Instead of reaching for it, he moved on, licking his way down her rib cage as he eased lower on the mattress. He paused to explore her navel.

She groaned and dug her fingers into his shoulders. "Nash...I want..."

"You'll get what you want," he murmured. Balanced on his forearm, he used his free hand to loosen her hold. Then he brought her hand to his mouth and made passionate love to it. He sucked on each finger and dipped his tongue into each crevice. He traced every line in her palm.

She began to tremble, and he wondered if she was responsive enough to come through suggestion alone. He had something else in mind, something he'd never tried before, but Bethany inspired him to be creative. He held on to her moist hand as he slid lower. The scent of her arousal made him long to taste her, but first...

Grasping her wrist, he drew her hand down between her thighs. "Show me how you touch yourself. Is it like this?" He took hold of her finger and rubbed it back and forth over her sweet little clit.

She groaned but didn't pull away. She was obviously desperate for a climax.

"Or like this?" He switched to a circular movement. "Like...that."

"Keep doing it, Bethany. Let me watch."

She continued the caress he'd coaxed her into, and her breathing grew rough with excitement.

"Don't stop. I'm going to help." His pulse raced as he slipped two fingers deep inside her. "You're so wet, so incredibly wet."

"Because I want—"

"I know. Come for me." He matched his strokes to her rhythm, and as she rubbed faster and harder, he increased his speed. The liquid sound he created nearly made him come, too. He wouldn't be able to play this game much longer.

He felt her contractions a split second before she cried out and arched upward. Slipping his hand free, he slid his shoulders under her raised hips. Then he settled his mouth over the entrance to all things wonderful. She was still riding the crest of pleasure, and he intended to keep her up there.

BETHANY'S FIRST CLIMAX nearly turned her inside out as promised. She was still shuddering in reaction when Nash brought his mouth into play. She sensed he was about to make good on his boast. Gasping and uttering wild, inarticulate noises, she gave herself up to the most sensuous round of oral sex she'd ever experienced.

He didn't mess around, this cowboy. He was coming to get her, and the tension built so quickly in her womb that in seconds he'd hurled her over the precipice into another shattering orgasm. She was just beginning to gather herself together when he began his assault again.

"I *can't!*"

He lifted his mouth long enough to say, "Sure you can," before seeking her essence once again. He'd breached her defenses and taken all she possessed. Now he demanded total surrender.

Heaven help her, she gave it—loudly, joyously, and yes, with much flailing around. A woman experiencing an orgasm this intense simply had to flail. When he finally lowered her hips and bestowed one parting kiss on her drenched curls, she sank to the bed in boneless ecstasy. He had, indeed, turned her inside out.

The mattress shifted.

"Please don't leave," she murmured.

"Wouldn't dream of it." Foil crinkled. "We still have unfinished business."

She struggled to find enough air in her lungs to tell him she was done. "You'll have to...finish it."

His chuckle was low and filled with desire. "Don't worry. I have enough momentum to carry both of us."

"Good."

He moved between her thighs. "A true gentleman wouldn't ask this of you." Bracing himself on his forearms, he probed gently with the tip of his penis. "But I've never claimed to be a true gentleman, and I need..." He sucked in a breath and rocked forward, burying himself deep. "This." He stayed still for several long moments before letting out his breath. Then he leaned down and kissed her gently. "Perfect."

Despite having three orgasms and feeling as if she had no more to give, Bethany found herself reacting to the delicious slide of his penis. "You feel good inside me."

"That's the general idea." He drew back a fraction and pushed home again. "If this didn't feel really good, the human race would have died out long ago."

The light had nearly faded from the room. Yet she

looked up at him, wanting to make that connection even though they couldn't see each other very well. "You're keeping a tight rein on yourself, aren't you?"

"Trying to. I don't want to jolt you out of your post-orgasmic haze if I can help it." He drew back and slid in again.

She found the energy to wiggle her hips. "You must want more than that. You've been on the verge of coming for quite a while. Aren't you ready to turn that bad boy loose?"

He squeezed his eyes shut. "You're a wicked woman, Bethany Grace. If you're not careful what you say, you're liable to find yourself being ridden like you've never been ridden before."

His words lit a flash fire that burned away her exhaustion and left desire beating a steady tattoo in her core. "You know what?" She wrapped her legs around his hips. "I'd like nothing better."

He hesitated, as if not quite believing what he'd heard. Then he groaned and his whole body tensed. "Damn, lady. I hope you know what you're asking for."

As she continued to gaze up at him, she clutched his muscled arms, loving the way they flexed beneath her fingers. "Do it, cowboy. Ride like the wind."

With a soft oath, he eased back, but this time he didn't return slowly. Oh, no. He shoved into her with a force that lifted her from the mattress.

Wow. She'd had no idea, but there was no time to think, only to feel. Nash radiated raw masculine power as instinct replaced logic. He seemed driven by the need to claim and possess, and she responded with primitive joy as she absorbed the pounding rhythm that shook her from the balls of her feet to the roots of her hair.

So this was how a man firmly planted in the natural world made love. The heat and intensity swept her along and she rose to meet each vigorous thrust. Panting, she urged him on, and he picked up the pace.

Their bodies became slick with sweat as they slammed together again and again. She hadn't expected to climax this time, but suddenly, there it was, and she was coming in glorious spirals of sensuality while he continued to pump into her, as though he couldn't get enough.

Then, with one last thrust and a groan that seemed torn from the depths of his soul, he shuddered in her arms. She held him close, murmuring soft words and stroking his back. Instinctively she knew that in responding to her tonight, he'd risked far more than she had.

He'd been hurt in ways that hadn't touched her, at least not yet. She'd never allowed herself to get serious enough about a man to contemplate marrying him. In some ways she'd protected herself from the worst kind of heartbreak. She'd never considered her choices to be cowardly, but they seemed that way now.

Nash hadn't been a coward, though. He'd flown into the heart of the storm and taken a beating. Sadly, her last book had been one of the lightning bolts that had nearly wiped him out.

Although she wouldn't take responsibility for that— his ex-wife could claim the honor—Nash deserved better. She didn't qualify because she wouldn't be sticking around long enough. But at least she wouldn't kick him in the teeth when she left.

Slowly he sank against her, although he kept most of his weight on his forearms. He nestled his head against her shoulder. "Incredible," he murmured.

"Yes." She continued to stroke his back. "Incredible."

"I'm afraid I'll fall asleep. I can't do that."

"Guess not."

"They'll expect me to come in at a reasonable hour."

She smiled. "It's like high school all over again with parents waiting up. Do you have a curfew?"

"No, but..."

"Someone will take note of when you get home."

"Yeah. I sleep in a bunkhouse. At least one of the hands will wake up if I come in late. Nothing will be said then, but tomorrow I'll face the comments and joking remarks."

"Do you care?"

"Not for myself." He propped his chin on his fist. "But I don't want them thinking anything they shouldn't about you."

She was touched by his chivalry. "I'm the one who started this by kissing you, Nash."

"No one will hear that from me."

"Does it matter? Even if I'm branded a loose woman, I'm not sticking around. If nobody connects me to the woman who writes motivational books, I'll just be the Grace girl who came back to straighten out her father's affairs, got it on with a local guy and left, never to be seen again."

"You have a point, but I still don't want to give anybody a reason to say something insulting about you. Then I'd have to deck them, and that's not—"

"You'd *fight* them?" She was stunned. "Why?"

He peered at her in the darkness. "How long have you been gone from this area?"

"I left when I was eighteen and haven't lived here

since then, which makes it about thirteen years. What does that have to do with anything?"

"Either you've forgotten how things work around here, or you never really knew. But in cowboy country, a man doesn't stand by and let others insult his wom— I mean, the person he's involved with. Well, unless he doesn't like her anymore and she deserves it. But even then, a guy's likely to stand up for her."

She caught the slip. He'd almost called her *his woman*. Chivalry was all well and good, but if it included possessive, paternalistic behavior, she would take a pass. "I appreciate the urge to defend my honor, Nash, but it's really not necessary. Besides, if you challenge someone to a fight because they said something about me, won't they get the wrong impression about our relationship?"

He was silent for a few moments as if considering that. "I suppose, which is why I can't fall asleep in your bed. If I show up back at the ranch before eleven, and I have some sawdust on my boots and maybe a little paint on my shirt, no one will imagine anything is going on between us."

Now it was her turn to think. Maybe she was being paranoid about how the Triple G looked. If she cleaned up the house and salvaged any keepsakes, something she could do during the day, maybe it wasn't so all-fired important for the exterior to get a face-lift. She wasn't trying to get top dollar, anyway.

If she was careful and cautioned the real estate agent to keep his or her mouth shut, no one would connect this place with her public persona. The less she had to worry about how this ranch looked on the outside, the more time she could spend in bed with Nash.

No, that wouldn't work. He'd already told her he

needed the money, and paying him for sex wouldn't fit either of their value systems. She'd already cut into tonight's income.

But now that she'd experienced being turned inside out by Nash Bledsoe, she wanted him to do it again. He might want that, too, which wouldn't leave him much time to work on her place. Unless they vowed to stop having sex, his paycheck would be adversely affected.

She took a deep breath. "I didn't consider all the ramifications of getting naked."

"That's okay. I did."

"You did? When?"

"During dinner, when I began to realize that we might end up like this."

"And what were your conclusions?"

He leaned down and placed a soft kiss on her mouth. "Before we talk about that, let's get dressed. We have things to discuss, and I don't know about you, but I'll think better if we both have clothes on."

She groaned. "Exactly. That's what I mean about not considering everything. I didn't realize that having sex tonight would mean we'd want to have it the rest of the week. Speaking strictly for me, of course. Maybe you don't—"

"Sweetheart, I definitely want to have sex all week. Never doubt it."

"But that presents a problem."

"Don't worry." He kissed her once more. "We'll work it out. I have an idea." He left the bed, headed into her bathroom and switched on the light.

She hoped he wasn't blinded by all that pink. Sitting up, she swung her legs to the floor. "What idea?" she called out.

"I'll tell you once we're both dressed."

"Sorry it's so pink in there." She stood and stretched. Wow, she was one satisfied woman.

"I can handle pink. Put on some clothes and I'll meet you in the dining room." A familiar squeak indicated that he'd turned on the faucet in the sink. The ancient pipes set up a racket, clanking and rattling until he turned off the water. "Good Lord. You need a plumber."

"I know." Feeling daring and sexy, she walked over to the bathroom and leaned against the doorjamb. "Have I found one?"

He met her gaze in the medicine cabinet mirror and grinned. "Lady, you've found yourself a jack-of-all-trades, master of none."

And there she was, ready to swoon again. "I can think of one thing you're a master of."

"Oh, yeah?" His grin widened.

"Mr. Bledsoe, you did indeed turn this girl inside out."

His grin faded as heat flickered in his blue eyes. "Glad to hear it. Now get out of here before you end up sitting on this pink counter with your legs in the air while I do you."

That visual prompted a burst of shocked laughter. "I don't know if I'd bend that way."

"You'd be surprised what you can do when you're highly motivated. But the vanity's so old we might break the damned thing. So get some clothes on. Please."

She hesitated, torn between finding out what his idea might be and experiencing bathroom-counter sex with him. She didn't really care if they broke the vanity.

"Go!"

That was when she noticed that he was gripping the

edge of the counter and had stepped back a little to make room for his growing erection.

"I really want to have a conversation with you." His tone was mild but his jaw twitched. "We need to be clear on a few things before we do this again."

"Right." She turned, hurried back into the bedroom and snatched up her clothes. She'd dress in the kitchen, away from temptation. The intensity of her craving for Nash, and his for her, was exciting. Scary, too.

He was right, though. They needed to be clear on a few things so that both of them would come out of this okay. No matter how glorious their sex life might turn out to be, it had a shelf life of one short week.

6

NASH DIDN'T WANT TO TAKE the time or deal with the discomfort of a cold shower, and he had some mental tricks for taming his buddy. Going through sports stats usually helped. But sure enough, his uncooperative brain superimposed the stats on Bethany's naked body.

Once the image popped into his head, it wouldn't leave. The stats rolled like movie credits, sliding over her breasts and down her tummy. Then they came to rest on…okay, stats weren't working for him tonight.

Maybe he should imagine himself in some crappy situation, like getting his truck stuck in the mud. Ah, mud. He pictured Bethany wrestling with him, her body slippery and agile until he finally pinned her and they had squishy, erotic sex. *Nice job, Bledsoe. Your cock is now harder than an ax handle. What else you got?*

With a loud curse, he stepped over to the shower and turned on the cold water. The clanking pipes covered the sound of more cussing as he subjected his overheated body to an icy spray. But it did the job.

He needed his wits about him when he made his offer to buy the ranch. Thinking of sex with Bethany might distract him and screw up the discussion before it had reached the conclusion he wanted. He also couldn't forget to tell her she was free to change her mind at the end of the week.

Knowing he had to add that part made him nervous, but it was the only fair way to approach what was a big decision for both of them. In fact, pushing her to decide tonight was neither fair nor smart. He should give her time to think about it.

After drying off with her very pink towel, he hung it back where he'd found it and walked into the bedroom to get dressed. The door into the kitchen was closed, but a light shone underneath. From the sound of dishes being scraped in the kitchen and the aroma of coffee brewing, he figured out that she wasn't waiting patiently in the dining room like he'd told her to. He should have known she wouldn't meekly follow his directions.

Well, good for her. Whenever he was agitated, like now, he had a bad habit of giving orders. Lindsay had called him on it, and in that area, she'd been absolutely justified in criticizing his behavior. Although he'd been working on that character flaw, apparently the luscious Miss Grace had stressed him to the point of reverting to his old bossy self.

After pulling on his briefs and jeans, he sat on the edge of her little bed to tug on his boots. During that operation he realized what a disaster he'd made of her bedroom. She'd had it fixed all neat and tidy, and he'd flung pillows and linens every which way. She brought out something in him that no other woman ever had, and he'd be damned if he knew why.

At first he'd been intrigued with the idea of storming the castle that was Bethany Grace, motivational guru.

Mission accomplished. She'd even said so. Yet instead of proclaiming mission accomplished and resting on his laurels, he wanted more.

Everything about her—the softness of her skin, the shape of her mouth, the luster of her hair, the curve of her hips, the scent of her body—drove him bat-shit crazy with lust. That hadn't happened to him before, not ever. He'd been attracted to women and enjoyed them immensely. He'd fallen in love, or thought he had, with Lindsay.

But this—this was something else. Maybe it was the ticking clock affecting him. No matter what, she'd be gone in a week. It could be that old scarcity model. Because she was only available to him a few hours a night for one precious week, he felt a sense of urgency, a need to make the most of it.

Whether or not they would act like crazed bunnies this week depended mostly on the outcome of their upcoming discussion. Originally he'd planned to talk about this over a bottle of wine. As he buttoned his shirt and tucked it into his jeans, he smiled.

The wine had served a different function, and he wasn't sorry. No matter what happened from here on out, he wouldn't ever regret what they'd just shared. As they said in sports, tonight was one for the record books.

After buckling his belt, he turned on her bedside lamp so he could straighten the room a little. He didn't put it all back the way she'd had it because he couldn't remember exactly how it had been and he wasn't much of an arranger. But he draped the top sheet and comforter over the bed and piled on the pillows so they were no longer on the carpet.

Finally, he walked to the door and opened it. She

stood at the sink, her hands deep in soapsuds. He'd halfway expected her to leap for the light switch because earlier she'd been so insistent that he not see the shabby kitchen.

But she stayed where she was and simply turned her head to smile at him. Once again, he didn't notice his surroundings at all. All he could see was her.

It was one of those moments that would stay with him for a long time. Although she was dressed in her sleeveless white blouse and gray capris, the clothes were rumpled from being on the floor. Knowing why they'd been on the floor made the outfit sexier than a negligee.

She'd finger-combed her hair, but she had some little cowlicks going on in back, no doubt caused by sweating and tossing her head around each time he made her come. She had no makeup left, but her flushed cheeks and bright eyes indicated that she was a woman who'd recently enjoyed some very good sex.

And perhaps the most appealing thing of all, the part of the presentation that made him long to wrap his arms around her and never let go, was her decision to have this discussion barefoot. Something about that implied trust. He was touched, turned on and wholly captured by this woman. He'd be wise not to let her know that, because then their situation could get really dicey.

"Coffee?" she asked.

"Love some."

"Brownies?"

"My favorite. Don't tell me you baked today, on top of everything else you did."

"Nope." She let the water out of the sink and grabbed a towel to wipe her hands. "I knew this would be a rough week, so besides buying groceries in Jackson, I hit a bakery and stocked up on goodies."

A rough week. Right. She'd just lost her father. Some people handled grief by getting it on with the nearest available partner. Well, if he served that purpose for her, he didn't really mind. It wasn't as if the sex could lead to anything, anyway.

He glanced around the kitchen. "What can I do?"

She opened the refrigerator and pulled out a white bakery box. The scent of chocolate came with it. "Carry these into the dining room. I could arrange them on a plate, but—"

"No need to dirty another dish." He took the box she gave him. "I'm happy to eat right out of this."

"Good. Me, too. Do you take anything in your coffee?"

"Just black."

She laughed. "I suppose that's the cowboy way."

"It used to be, but if you look in the bunkhouse refrigerator you'll find all kinds of flavored creamers. Cowboys have gone soft these days."

"Except for you."

"Yes, ma'am. Nothing about me is soft." He waggled his eyebrows at her.

"Listen to you! Weren't you the one who wanted to have a strictly platonic discussion? And now you're bringing up the subject of your hard body, which naturally leads to thoughts of your hard—"

"Sorry, sorry, sorry." But he wasn't, not really. He had fun teasing her. "You're right. I'll go into the dining room with the brownies and promise not to say anything suggestive for the next...oh, let's say twenty minutes."

"We can complete our discussion in twenty minutes?"

"I'd like to." He exited to the dining room through the open pocket door. "Because then we can move on to other more exciting activities."

"Nash."

"What?" He set the box on the table and turned back toward the kitchen. "I meant things like checking over the property and discussing repairs. That kind of exciting."

"Sure you did." She came in carrying two steaming mugs of coffee. "I'm having flashbacks to high school when I used to hear you and your buddies in the halls bragging about your…attributes."

"They bragged." He fought to keep from laughing. "I didn't have to."

"Oh, my God. You must need a wheelbarrow to carry around that ego."

"Let's just say that my athletic cup had to be custom-made." That was a complete lie, but he managed to tell it with a straight face.

"It did not." She set down the mugs at their respective places and peered at him. "Did it?"

He started to laugh. "No, it didn't. I told you earlier that I'm standard-issue."

"I would disagree with that claim."

"You would?" He was male enough to enjoy hearing that.

"Now you're fishing."

"Can't blame me for that. You're my first in many moons. It's nice to hear that I've still got what it takes."

She gazed at him thoughtfully. "How many moons?"

"Well, I'd have to count, but I haven't had sex with anyone since Lindsay."

Her eyes widened. "How long have you been divorced?"

"Technically, about twenty-four hours. But I left Sacramento last August. The legal process dragged on for months, but the relationship ended last summer."

"And you haven't dated anyone since you came back?"

He shook his head. "I wanted to give myself some time."

"I wish I'd known." She blew out a breath. "I mean, you're Nash Bledsoe. Naturally I assumed that you'd come back here and pick up where you left off."

"First of all, those women are all married now, and second of all, why do you wish you'd known?"

"I would have thought twice about having sex with you, in case you might attach too much importance to it."

That stung, even though he understood why she'd said it. She was a psychologist, after all. "I'm not an emotional cripple who needs coddling, Bethany. When I went into that bedroom with you, I knew the score. You'll be gone next week. In some ways, that makes you the perfect rebound woman. You can help me get my groove back without any complications." He sounded extremely convincing, if he did say so himself.

She seemed taken aback. "I hadn't thought of it that way, but that makes perfect sense." She sounded almost disappointed, though.

Interesting. "I told you I'd considered the ramifications."

"So you did. And you have a plan to propose."

"I do." He moved to her chair. "Have a seat. Let's find out if my persuasive abilities extend beyond the bedroom." He helped her into her chair and walked around to his.

"This feels like a business meeting."

"That's because it is." He sat down and picked up his mug of coffee.

"I've never done business with a man who's seen me naked."

He smiled at her over the rim of his mug. "That only serves to make the deal more interesting."

"You're a man of many roles—cowboy, handyman, deal maker."

"Don't forget *superlative lover*."

"As if I could. I don't know if I can talk business with someone who gets my panties wet."

He almost choked on his coffee. He swallowed the hot liquid and stared at her. "Now?"

"Of course. I'm like one of Pavlov's dogs. You give me that special glance and, whoosh, my panties are wet."

"I probably shouldn't be happy about that, but I am. I might have had that effect on other women, but they've never told me."

"Trust me, Nash, you've had that effect on other women. I can guarantee it. For whatever reason, they were too proud or too shy to let you know. I'm not too proud or too shy, although normally I can be both. It must be the multiple orgasms that have loosened my tongue, along with every other muscle in my body. You're better than a deep tissue massage, my friend."

He allowed himself to bask in the admiration shining in her gray eyes. "Thank you."

"You're welcome. And although I can't imagine doing business with someone who's recently had his head between my thighs and his mouth on my hoo-ha, I'm dying of curiosity about this deal of yours."

He grinned at her. How could he do anything else when she was so completely adorable? He hoped she'd go for the concept, but if not, he'd had an unforgettable experience being here tonight.

He took another sip of his coffee and considered how best to broach the subject. In the end he decided on simplicity. "I want to buy the Triple G."

She blinked. Clearly this wasn't what she'd expected him to say. "Oh."

Now that it was on the table, his heart thudded with anxiety. He wanted this more than he'd realized. "I don't have a big down payment, but if you require more than I have, I may be able to borrow some from Jack. There are programs for first-time homebuyers and I should qualify. It's not as crazy as it sounds. I'll figure out the money part."

"I'm not worried about—"

"If you sold to me, you wouldn't have to be so concerned about how the property appears to a prospective buyer. I know how it looks, and I don't care. It's a nice size for starting out, and it abuts the Last Chance, which belongs to one of my best friends. The location is awesome for me."

"So you'd live here?" The idea seemed to bewilder her.

"That's generally what a person does when they buy a place, unless it's strictly for investment. I want to live here. I want to build it back up, get horses, maybe a goat or two, and—"

"A goat?"

"Sure. There's this one goat at the Last Chance named Hornswaggled, although we all call him Horny. He's an amazing animal. If we have a horse that's acting up, we put Horny in the stall for a few days, and the horse settles right down. He has a special friend named Doozie, a mare that Gabe bought, but he's a calming influence on all the horses. Yep, I'd definitely invest in at least one goat."

She continued to stare off into space, as if she couldn't comprehend having him buy this place. And yet she'd been planning to sell it all along, so it couldn't be the idea of selling that had her so distracted. No, it had to be the idea of selling it to *him*.

Although he still wasn't sorry about having sex with her, he had a tiny regret that he hadn't mentioned the possibility of buying the ranch before they'd walked into her bedroom. He'd been about to say something when she'd taken the bull by the horns and admitted to craving his body. Some guys might have managed to refuse that offer, but he hadn't.

Besides, rejecting her sexual advances would have hurt his cause, not helped it. A spurned woman wasn't likely to sell her home with generous terms to the guy who had spurned her. No, the thing that had landed him in this mess was easy to identify.

Toward the end of dinner, they'd both announced they had confessions to make. Being a courteous cowboy, he'd allowed her to go first. Once she'd confessed her interest in him, he couldn't very well change the subject and offer to buy her ranch. That confession had been shoved to the back burner.

He'd hoped it hadn't been removed from the stove

altogether, but he had to face that possibility. Before dinner, he'd been just a guy with an unspoken desire to buy her place. Now he was the guy who'd given her four orgasms in her childhood bedroom. Selling the ranch to him carried a lot more emotional baggage, and he had to accept responsibility for loading up the suitcases.

"I realize you will have to think about this," he said.

She nodded and finally she met his gaze. "Yes, I will."

"I'd like to give you all the time in the world, but neither of us has a lot of time."

"That's for sure."

"I don't want to pressure you, but whichever way you go will affect how I approach the repairs and whether I do any at all, so I really can't start until you decide."

She considered that for a moment. Finally she nodded. "So if you're buying the place, we're no longer employer and employee. You won't need to worry about repairs because you'll do them later to suit you."

"Exactly."

"But if no one knows about our arrangement, you can continue to come over here each night whether you're fixing the place or not."

He hesitated. "I hadn't thought that far ahead, but yes, I could, if that's what you want."

"After what happened in that bedroom? A girl would have to be crazy in the head not to want more of that kind of action."

He should be flattered, but he had an uneasy feeling about the direction the conversation was taking. "Thanks."

"You're welcome. This is a devilishly clever scheme, Nash. You've set it up so that I can either accept you as a buyer and have a fantastic lover for six nights, or reject your offer and pay you handyman wages while hoping there's time for a quick roll in the hay between carpentry jobs."

He stared at her and then he looked away, upset with himself for not realizing how his offer could be seen as coercion. "I swear I didn't intend to use sex as leverage."

"I believe you," she said gently. "But whether you intended to or not, it works out that way, doesn't it?"

He blew out a breath and tried to think how to salvage the situation. "It doesn't have to. I'll find you a handyman. He won't have to know that he's working for a bestselling author. I'll get someone who can work during the day. Then everything can be separated out. Whether you sell to me or not is up to you. Whether we have sex is up to you. No catch-22 involved."

She gazed at him. "You'll give up income if you bring in someone else."

"I know. Can't be helped. I won't put you in a position where you feel you have to sell to me."

"If this other handyman makes the place look amazing, he could raise the value beyond your price point."

"I'll take that chance." He hated the thought that came to him next, but he knew it had to be said. "In fact, we can't have sex anymore, either. Although I wouldn't mean to soften you up so you'll sell to me, it could turn out that way. I don't want you to think back to this sale and wonder if your judgment had been affected by all that good loving."

"So you're prepared to give up income and fantastic sex on the slight chance that accepting either of those things would jeopardize your chances of buying the Triple G."

He nodded. Damn, this week wasn't going to be any fun at all.

"I'm impressed with your ethics, Nash." She picked a brownie out of the box. "Please, help yourself."

"Don't mind if I do." A brownie was a poor substitute for six nights in her bed, but it was a safer bet. He took a moist chocolate square and bit into it while avoiding watching Bethany eat hers. Inevitably he'd be turned on if he did, and that wasn't a good idea now that he'd sworn off having sex with her ever again.

She finished her brownie and dusted off her hands. "Has it occurred to you that by not having sex with me, you might tip the scales the other way?"

He swallowed his last bite. "How so?"

"You gave me a taste of your manly charms, and now you're proposing to withdraw those charms."

He groaned. "Are you saying I can't win?"

"No. I'm saying we have a complicated little deal going on here, and we both need time to think it through. Tell you what. I'll get a real estate agent out here tomorrow, before anyone does anything to the place beyond the flowers I put out and whatever cleaning I do inside the house."

"If you call Morgan Chance, don't tell her you're thinking of selling to me. I'd rather nobody knows that just yet."

"Who's Morgan? I take it she's connected to the family, but I don't remember hearing her name before."

"She's Gabe's wife. She has an office in Shoshone, so she could get here quicker than someone from Jackson. And she's good."

"Then I'll call her. Come back tomorrow night and

I'll tell you what she says. Then you'll have a figure to work with."

"You could text me the figure."

"I know."

"Bethany, you tempt me like no other woman ever has. And so—"

"I do?"

"Yes, so if I have to swear off having sex with you, I'd rather not meet face-to-face anymore. It's easier that way."

She smiled. "Like *no other woman?* Nash, you must have had lots of women in your bed."

"A few."

"Don't be modest. I've heard the rumors. I don't understand why I would affect you this way. Maybe it's because you were unhappy in your marriage, plus your abstinence these past months, because I'm not that special."

"You're extremely special, but that doesn't explain my reaction. You're beautiful, but I admit I've been with beautiful women before. There's something about you—the way you move, the way you smell, the sound of your voice—the total package jacks me up something fierce. So text me, okay?"

She shook her head. "I want you to come over. Neither one of us should be kept dangling this week. I'll let you know my decision tomorrow night, and we can take it from there."

He studied her while he tried to figure out what she was saying. In the end, he couldn't. "What do you mean by *take it from there?*"

"If I decide to sell you the ranch, we can have sex. If I decide not to sell you the ranch, we can have sex.

In other words, once the decision is made, we can have sex."

"Oh." His cock twitched. He cared which decision she made, of course. He cared a whole hell of a lot. But either way, he'd be assured of another night with her. Six more nights, in fact, unless he loused this up somehow. "I can live with that."

"Good. Now go home before I jump your bones."

"I need to load up that chair first."

"No, leave it. I sort of like looking at it now."

"Why?"

"Ever since I set fire to that recliner, my life has become a lot more interesting."

"Mine, too." He stood and grabbed his hat from the back of a chair. "See you tomorrow night. What time?"

"Make it eight. I don't want to waste time on dinner."

He sucked in a breath as his cock responded further.

"See you later, cowboy."

Not trusting himself to stay another second, he walked out of the house, down the porch steps and over to his truck. The fire retardant he'd sprayed on this morning had dried on the black mound that used to be a recliner, and it gleamed in the moonlight. Funny how something so ugly had the power to change his life so much.

7

MORGAN CHANCE SHOWED UP right at ten the next morning driving a dark green SUV with mud spatters on the fenders. Bethany went out to meet her because she'd discovered the doorbell didn't work. Besides, she wanted to take Morgan on a tour of the outbuildings before bringing her into the house.

Although Bethany had been up early cleaning, the place still didn't meet her standards. The outbuildings were old and dilapidated, but their appearance didn't embarrass her the way the house did. Maybe that was because her mom had been such a neat freak and while she'd been alive, she'd kept everything scrubbed even if it was worn. Her mother would have hated for a stranger to see the neglect that had set in during the past eighteen months.

Morgan turned out to be a buxom redhead with a great smile. A couple of car seats in the back of the SUV suggested she and Gabe had kids. Bethany was used to meeting women her age with kids because so many had them by now. She was the exception—a single lady with no children.

Maybe she never would have kids. First she'd have to find the right guy, and so far he'd been AWOL. An image of Nash flashed into her head, but that meant nothing. Images of Nash had been interrupting her thoughts every waking moment since he'd left the night before. He was one hot dude.

Morgan climbed out, large sunglasses perched on the bridge of her freckled nose, a purse over her shoulder and an electronic gizmo in her hand. It looked like the newest tablet, maybe even the one Bethany had been considering but hadn't bought yet. Morgan extended her free hand and introduced herself.

"Thanks for coming on such short notice." Bethany liked Morgan's warm, firm handshake.

"No problem. I've discovered in ranching country the sales are few and far between, but when they come, they're substantial."

"Not if you're talking about the Triple G, I'm afraid. It's seen better days. And it's small."

"Yes, but the view is wonderful and lots of clients prefer something smaller." Morgan glanced around, pausing briefly at the large black lump that used to be the recliner. But she didn't comment and her gaze moved on. "I see what you mean about the upkeep, but it's possible someone would buy it for the land alone."

Bethany's stomach flipped. If someone bought it for the land, it went without saying that they'd tear down the buildings and start over. Although such a plan was completely logical, the concept made her queasy. Apparently she cared about this old wreck of a place, after all.

Morgan pushed her sunglasses to the top of her head. She had gorgeous eyes, a startling turquoise color. Her expression softened in understanding. "You grew up here, right?"

Bethany nodded. Silly, but her throat was too tight to speak.

"Are you sure you want to sell it? Because I can't guarantee that the new owners will leave the buildings intact."

Bethany cleared her throat. "I have to sell it. I have too much going on in my life to worry about maintaining this ranch."

"You could hire somebody."

Once again she thought of Nash. If she didn't sell it, would he consider living here and keeping it up for her? No, that wouldn't work. She and Nash had different dreams and they'd be better off making a clean break when the week was over.

She glanced at Morgan. "No, I'm sure I want to sell it and forget it." Even as she said that, she knew the chances of forgetting this place were slim. It was still in her blood. She could feel it.

"Okay. And even though a buyer might take down the buildings, they might not, too. Some people love things to be weathered and rustic. I'm just warning you, so you're not grief-stricken if you come back and find it all changed."

"I won't come back." She especially wouldn't if Nash bought it. She couldn't picture him living on this ranch alone. Once he had a place of his own, he'd go looking for a woman to share it with. Bethany didn't care to drive in and discover some other chick tending flowers on the porch and maybe bouncing Nash's kid on her hip.

"All righty, then. Where would you like to start?"

"How about the barn?"

"That works." Morgan was dressed in boots and jeans, but she wore a yellow scoop-necked T-shirt in deference to the warmth of the morning.

Knowing she'd be tramping around the property, Bethany had dug out a pair of boots from her closet. She hadn't worn them in ages. They had to be at least fifteen years old, and the minute she'd put them on, she'd felt like a teenager again. It wasn't a bad feeling, surprisingly enough.

"I'm sorry about your father," Morgan said as they walked toward the barn, which was about fifty yards from the house.

Bethany sighed. "He didn't have a very good end, I'm afraid. And I didn't make it here in time."

"That's rough."

"I don't think he wanted me here. We weren't close, and he kept saying everything was fine. I knew it wasn't, but I was afraid to come back and find...well, this." She swept an arm to encompass the horse barn, the tractor barn, the chicken coop and various corrals.

"It must be heartbreaking for you."

"My dad didn't maintain this part very well at the best of times. The house, though—that's where the heartbreak sets in." She paused before the barn door. It had been open when she'd pulled in yesterday, so she'd seen no point in closing it and possibly trapping whatever wild creatures might be living in there. "Let me go first. I haven't been inside yet."

"Don't blame you."

Bethany stepped through the door and listened. Silence. Then she heard fluttering and glanced up. Birds had nested in the rafters, which were filled with cobwebs. She was glad she hadn't closed in the birds. They might have babies by now. A mouse scurried across the floor and disappeared through an open stall door.

The barn still smelled faintly of hay, but the last horse had been sold months ago, so any remaining manure had dried up and lost its scent. She chose not to inspect the tack hanging on a wall, or the three saddles resting on sawhorses. If mice had taken over, they'd probably chewed the leather.

"I think it's safe to come in," she called over her shoulder. "I don't see or hear anything dangerous."

Morgan walked through the door. "I checked out the roof a little. From the ground, it doesn't look too bad. Maybe it needs some patching, but I couldn't see any obvious damage. Replace the hinges on the door, sweep the place out, get yourself a cat, and this barn would be workable."

"Good to know." Bethany congratulated herself on her casual reply. The longer she stayed in the barn, the more sentimental she became. She'd had a horse stabled in this barn. Gingerbread had been twenty-five when her father bought the gelding for Bethany's sixth birthday. She'd ridden him for ten years before he got into some bad hay and that was that.

She hadn't thought about Gingerbread in a long time, but she remembered sunlit rides through fields of purple lupine. Sometimes her dad would come along and occasionally her mom would, too. A few times she'd invited friends from school, but mostly she'd ridden alone. And she'd loved it.

"I count six stalls," Morgan said. "That's plenty for a ranch this size."

"We never filled them all, either. Three horses were the most we ever had at one time. My dad thought he'd enjoy owning a ranch, but the reality of it was never really his thing."

"It isn't for everyone. So, shall we move on?"

"Sure." She reminded herself that Morgan was here to assess the property and get on with her day. Bethany could take a stroll down memory lane later.

The tractor barn contained one rusty tractor and her dad's aging blue pickup. Seeing that old truck brought tears to her eyes, but she blinked them away. Not now.

"If either the truck or the tractor run, you could consider selling them with the ranch," Morgan said.

"I'll check that out. If they don't run, I'll arrange to have them towed."

"Okay. Once again, this building seems sound. A little work on the roof, maybe some fresh paint, and it would be serviceable. It's less critical than the barn because the vehicles won't try to get out."

Bethany smiled. "Thanks. This tour could use a touch of humor. Sorry if I've been too grim."

"I know it must be hard, but you're holding up great." Morgan gave Bethany's shoulder a squeeze.

"Happiness is a choice." Bethany said it without thinking. Whoops.

"You've got that right." Morgan paused to look at her as if trying to remember something. "There's something familiar about you, Bethany. I've thought so ever since I arrived."

"I went to school here, so if you did, too, that could be it." She decided a change of scenery might sidetrack this discussion. "Ready to see the house?"

"Absolutely." Morgan walked beside Bethany toward the shabby little ranch house. "I don't think it was school I know you from. My folks moved around a lot. Still do, in fact. I was only here for one semester. But…wait a minute, it's coming to me. Bethany Grace! That's where I read Happiness Is a Choice. You wrote *Living with Grace!* Your picture's on the dustcover of the book, and so is that quote."

Bethany sighed. Trust her to locate the one person in town besides Nash Bledsoe who'd heard of her. "Yep, I am and it is."

"My mother *loves* that book! She gave it to all us kids for Christmas last year. She will be so excited that I've actually met you."

Dread swirled in Bethany's tummy. "Does your mom live here?"

"No. Well, my folks spend part of the year here, but they're vagabonds. Right now they're over in Ojai, California, at a spiritual retreat. I'll bet my mom's read every motivational book ever published, but she really liked yours."

Bethany knew better than to ask if Morgan had read it. She'd mentioned that it was a Christmas gift, and this was June. She hadn't said a single word about how much *she* had enjoyed it. That was okay with Bethany. Not everyone was into self-help.

But she needed to do some damage control. "Morgan, I have a favor to ask. Could you please not tell anyone who I am? I mean, you can say something to your mom, since she doesn't live here. But the Triple G is… not something I want the world to hear about, at least not when it looks like this."

Morgan nodded. "You're a public figure, so I understand completely."

"Thanks. I appreciate your discretion." The tension eased from Bethany's shoulders. "I can imagine the reaction going one of two ways, neither of them good. Either the media will play up the irony of me having a father who wasn't *living with grace,* or it will praise me for overcoming the handicap of growing up in depressing circumstances. My dad wasn't perfect, but I don't want his story sensationalized."

"Of course you don't. Tell you what. I won't mention you to my mom until the ranch is either fixed up or sold. The sooner one of those two things happens, the better. It's always possible someone else will recognize you before you accomplish that."

"Nash Bledsoe knows." Bethany didn't feel right guaranteeing Morgan's silence without telling her about Nash. "His ex was a fan of my books, and he put two and two together."

Morgan's jaw dropped. "The Wicked Witch of the West read your books?"

"You knew her?"

"Not personally, but Nash has said enough that I'm sure I wouldn't care for her at all. If half of what I've heard is true, she must not have absorbed your message."

"Oh, she picked up on Happiness Is a Choice, all right, and she clubbed him over the head with it whenever he objected to her patronizing behavior. He was supposed to be happy being her whipping boy."

"Sadistic bitch." Morgan glanced at Bethany. "So Nash knows who you are, but he's okay with it? He's not blaming you for contributing to his misery?"

"He'd love to, but he's a better man than that." Instantly Bethany wished she'd made the comment with less warmth.

Morgan's gaze flickered. "He's a good guy." She

paused. "He tells everyone that's the last time he'll hook up with a woman who has more money than he does."

"You can't blame him." She wasn't sure if Morgan was warning her or protecting Nash, but either way, the comment underscored Nash's intentions toward her. He was in it for the sex. In a way, she was relieved to know he'd guard his heart.

"I'm glad you hired him to work on the place," Morgan said. "He came out of the divorce broke, and he could use the money. It's crazy that he happened to know who you are, but I'll bet you won't bump into anyone else who recognizes you. The people around here don't seem prone to reading motivational books." She winced. "Sorry. That didn't come out right. I meant—"

"It's okay, Morgan." Bethany laughed. "I'm glad they don't. I'd rather be anonymous right now." As she said that she realized how much she'd enjoyed not being a celebrity for the past twenty-four hours. Her success thrilled her, but being in the public eye took some getting used to. "Come on in the house. I have coffee and brownies."

"Yum." Morgan followed her up the creaky porch steps. "If I can have a few minutes on my tablet, I may be able to give you a rough idea of a good asking price before I leave."

"That would be awesome." She had another thought. "Do you suppose the Chances are interested? I hadn't considered that until just now. Maybe they want to increase their acreage."

She wondered if the idea had occurred to Nash. He was loyal to that family and if they wanted the ranch, he might back off. The possibility made her sad. Yeah, she wanted to help him make his dream come true. He'd had that kind of effect on her.

"I don't know if they're interested or not, but if you're at all worried that I might let my connection to them affect my obligation to get you the best price, then I'd be happy to suggest a different agent." Morgan didn't sound at all upset. She was obviously a real pro.

"Heavens, no." Bethany held the screen door open for her. "The Chances have a great reputation around here for being straight shooters. I'd trust a member of the Chance family way more than some real estate agent I don't know."

"Thanks." Morgan gave her a smile as she walked inside. "That's great to hear. The coffee smells wonderful, by the way."

Bethany had made the coffee for two reasons. Having it available was a gracious gesture and she'd written a whole book about gracious gestures. But the aroma also helped disguise the stale odor that permeated most of the house.

Morgan paused to study the living room. "Crown molding and a pressed tin ceiling. I'll bet this could be pretty."

"It used to be. Take out the trashed sofa, the easy chair and that cheap coffee table, put up new window coverings, replace the carpet…"

"I'd bet dollars to donuts there's hardwood under there."

"Could be. I was young when the carpet went in, but I have a vague memory of wooden floors."

Morgan's eyes lit with enthusiasm. "Are you committed to replacing the carpet?"

Until now, Bethany hadn't thought about it, but Morgan's comment made her realize how gratifying it would be to get rid of the hideous, smelly shag. "Yes."

"So you'll be ripping the old stuff out, for sure, then?"

"Yes."

"Excellent. If you can locate an X-Acto knife, we can find out what's under there."

"Dirt. And God knows what other disgusting stuff you don't want to know about. Besides, you'll mess up your clothes."

"That's why I wear jeans, boots and sensible shirts. I couldn't get away with this outfit in the big city, but here it works. Dirt and dead bugs don't scare me. Hardwood floors will add to the value of the house."

"I suppose." At least she'd vacuumed the carpet, although her mother's old machine no longer worked very well.

"A good hardwood floor might even save the house from being torn down. Plus I live for these kinds of discoveries."

"Really?"

Morgan laughed. "I know. I'm a real estate geek."

"Let me see what tools I can find in the kitchen. Come on back." She led Morgan through the dining room. Anything that would help save the house from the wrecking ball was worth the time. She was also impressed with Morgan's determination, which was a good quality in a salesperson.

Morgan smiled as they passed through the dining room. "Oh, I love this space."

"Thanks. Me, too." After last night, it would never seem the same. This was where she'd kissed Nash, right before they'd made a beeline for her bedroom.

"You've been here such a short time, but you've already put your stamp on the house with fresh flowers, candles and a nice tablecloth. I'll bet none of that was here when you arrived."

"The tablecloth was, and the candlesticks." Bethany continued on into the kitchen. Those items would always remind her of Nash Bledsoe, fantasy cowboy and lover extraordinaire. That meant she probably shouldn't keep them. Opening the kitchen junk drawer, she rummaged around and came up with an X-Acto knife. "Aha!"

"Perfect. Is it okay if I put my stuff on your kitchen table? I want both hands free so I can tear into that carpet."

"Go ahead." Bethany couldn't help smiling. "You really get into this, don't you?"

"I do." She took the knife and marched back into the living room. "My parents and eight kids lived in a hippie van my entire childhood. My parents and some of my siblings loved it. I hated it. So every home, mine or someone else's, is precious to me."

"I imagine it would be." And the longer they talked about this house, the more Bethany acknowledged that she was more attached to it than she'd realized. Selling it wouldn't be as easy as she'd first thought.

Morgan knelt by the nearest wall and began to cut through the ancient carpet. It was so threadbare that the job didn't take long. Caught up in Morgan's excitement, Bethany sank down next to her.

When Morgan had made a cut about a foot long and six inches on each side, she reached under the flap of carpeting and pulled. Dust flew, and they both coughed.

Morgan waved the dust away, ripped through the flimsy padding and gave a shout of triumph.

"Hardwood! Oak, it looks like." She grinned at Bethany. "You *have* to tear this carpet out and get the floors polished. It would be criminal to put new carpeting in. I'd offer to help take out the old stuff, but my daughter Sarah's second birthday is in a couple of weeks and it's shaping up to be a frickin' coronation, plus I'm nursing little Jonathan, who just turned three months, and…"

"Don't even think about helping," Bethany said. "This is my week to settle everything at the Triple G, and if you can take care of the listing, I'll do the rest."

"I can definitely take care of the listing. And your ace in the hole is Nash. He could have this carpet out of here in no time. He's handy."

"Right." She got to her feet and hoped Morgan wouldn't notice that she was blushing. "Although I was planning to assign him to outside renovation first." Sort of. Unless other, more personal activities took him away from that chore.

"How you make use of his time is up to you, but this floor will be a major selling point so I'd suggest bringing Nash in here to help you."

"It's a good idea." Bethany was desperate to change the subject. "So, why don't I pour some coffee while you crunch the numbers for me?"

"Sounds like a plan." Standing, Morgan dusted off her hands. "Someone put a lot of love into building this house. Was it your parents?"

"No. They bought it already built. I don't remember too much because I was so little, but I think the owners were an older couple who had to move to a warmer climate for the wife's health."

"Well, they left behind a gem. Taking a diamond in the rough and polishing it is so much fun."

Bethany led the way back into the kitchen. "I'm not sure how much polishing I can do in a week. I'd consider hiring more people, but that increases the odds that somebody will figure out who I am. Nash has agreed to keep quiet, and I know you will, so I feel fairly secure at this point."

"Then I recommend that you have Nash do the bare minimum outside and concentrate his efforts in here."

"Okay, I will." Bethany busied herself getting out mugs, sugar and cream while she fought the urge to giggle.

She'd already decided that Nash should concentrate his efforts inside the house. The activity she'd had in mind had nothing to do with renovation, though. Morgan would be expecting miracles, and if Bethany and Nash hoped to renovate this house while also having wild monkey sex every night, it would take several miracles.

8

NASH SPENT A GOOD PART of the day teaching two of the
Last Chance Youth Program boys the correct way to
muck out a stall. Eddie was a blond and pudgy thirteen-
year-old who was eager to please. The other kid, a skinny,
tattooed fourteen-year-old who insisted on being called
Ace, had major attitude. But Ace was careful not to cross
the line into open insolence, as if he knew how much
swagger he could get away with before being sent home.

Dealing with the two contrasting personalities on
the same work detail was a challenge, but Nash discovered he liked it. Both boys obviously yearned for a
male role model, and when Nash caught them picking
up his mannerisms, he smiled to himself. Imitation was
the sincerest form of flattery.

Lindsay hadn't been able to have kids, and had convinced him that was just as well. He'd bought into her
rationalizations, especially after he'd begun to worry
whether the marriage would last. Now that he looked
back on it, he understood that he'd been worried about
that from the get-go, but he'd been slow to admit defeat.

Now he was thirty-five, past the age when a lot of

guys had kids, but that didn't mean he couldn't still consider it if he found the right woman. Once he had his own place he could start thinking along those lines. For now, he had these eight boys to practice on.

He'd gotten an unexpected kick out of that. He'd relished the mental challenge of trying to outthink his two charges today. They could be incredibly funny, and they'd obviously loved making him crack up. They could also be achingly vulnerable and oblivious to the fact that they'd exposed their innermost secrets.

He looked forward to describing the day's activities to Bethany because he knew she'd be interested. That wasn't his main interest in going back over there, of course. He ached to make love to her again, and kept checking the time once the day's activities wound down.

Surprisingly, he wasn't as eager to hear Morgan's estimate on the Triple G's value as he'd expected to be. If he ended up buying the ranch, taking possession of it would coincide with Bethany leaving. Intellectually he understood that, but emotionally he was a long way from accepting it.

He'd get to that point eventually. But not tonight. As he drove over to the Triple G in the golden light of a brilliant sunset, a couple of his own condoms tucked in his jeans pocket, he had to consciously ease up on the gas pedal because his natural urge was to floor it. The washboard road slowed him down some, but he took that too fast anyway and his truck rattled in protest.

The previous night, he'd chosen his clothes so they'd be nice enough to eat dinner in and old enough to make repairs in. Tonight he'd opted for a worn pair of jeans, serviceable boots and a Western shirt with the sleeves rolled back. If she was true to her word, it would all come off. The thought of that caused the crotch of his jeans to pinch.

Although he halfway expected she might come out on the porch when she heard his truck, he hadn't anticipated that she'd be standing in the middle of the yard waiting as he hit the brakes and turned off the engine. She wore navy running shorts and a red halter top that made her look like summer itself.

A wiser man might have taken his time climbing down and walking over to her. But clearly he wasn't very wise, because he tossed his hat on the seat and leaped from the truck, leaving the door hanging open. She ran across the dirt yard and he met her halfway, catching her up in his arms and laughing as she wrapped her bare legs around his hips. He supported her by cupping her firm behind, and then he kissed her for all he was worth.

A separation of less than twenty-four hours seemed like days, and he couldn't get enough of her mouth. His cock swelled, and he knew where this kiss was leading. Carrying her, he started for the house.

He made it up the porch steps, across the porch and through the screen door. She pulled frantically at his clothes, and he doubted they'd get all the way to her bedroom before the action started. She'd popped all the snaps on his shirt by the time they'd staggered inside.

He knew better than to take her on the floor in here. Although she'd instructed him to ignore this room the previous night, he'd noticed the stained carpet and shabby furniture. The way she was moaning, though, she'd have an orgasm before they reached her bedroom, and he wanted to be inside her when she did.

So he made a command decision and backed her up

against the wall nearest the door. She must have caught on pretty quick, because once her back was against the wall, she stopped working on his shirt and started unfastening his belt. He managed to hold her one-handed, which took more strength than he'd known he had, but that allowed him to fish out the condom from his pocket. Apparently desperation made him stronger.

And eagerness made her faster. She'd freed him from his briefs and sheathed his bad boy in a time that might be a world record, if they had competitions for condom application. He was grateful for her speed when he realized that her running shorts stretched and she wore nothing underneath.

The way her breasts were heaving under the halter top, he suspected she was edging close to a climax, so he wasted no time in sliding home. That single thrust was all it took. She arched her back and convulsed around him as she gasped in pleasure.

He pumped slowly, drawing out the moment. As she started to settle down, he shifted the angle and drove deeper.

Her eyes flew open. *"Oh."*

"You didn't think I'd let you get away with just one, did you?"

She held his gaze. "I missed you."

"Same here." He pushed deeper and she opened to him, lifting toward him in total surrender. "Missed this, too."

"Uh-huh." Her breathing quickened. "Thought… about it."

"All day?" He increased the pace, daring her to keep up with him.

"Yes." She met him stroke for stroke and began to pant.

"Me, too. Imagined this. Burying my cock in you over and over."

"So good." She groaned. "Nash, I'm…"

"I know." Joy surged within him. "I can feel you tensing."

"Come with me."

"Love to." As the waves of her orgasm flowed over him, he let go. *Amazing.* Abandoning the last shred of control, he gave himself up to hot bursts of pleasure that seemed to go on…and on…and on. Her spasms milked him, leaving him gasping and trembling with the force of his response.

They clung to each other for long moments, and their ragged breathing was the only sound filling the silence. Nash wasn't sure what to say, what to do. He'd effectively bared his soul by letting her know how much he craved her. But she'd returned the favor. She craved him just as much.

Finally she leaned her head against the wall. "It's never been like this."

He was touched by her honesty. She didn't have to say that, but she'd said it anyway. "Not for me, either."

"Bummer."

He had to smile because he agreed. Finding sex that was so right when the relationship was so wrong could correctly be labeled a bummer. He took a deep breath. "Or."

"Or?"

"Or we could accept this interlude as a gift and cherish it while we can."

"Well, that's philosophical. Thank you very much, Zen Master."

"Hey." He leaned forward and brushed his mouth over hers. "Happiness is a—"

"Don't you dare quote me to myself, Nash Bledsoe. Not when your pride and joy is right where I could put it in a hammerlock."

"I was just—"

"Being obnoxious." She opened her eyes and smiled at him. "I guess you're allowed, all things considered. You've probably been hoping to deliver that line ever since you drove in here yesterday and found out who I was."

He grinned. "Maybe."

"Well, happiness *is* a choice and so is finding yourself in traction because you slipped a disk doing something you should have known was potentially hazardous. I vote we move this party to a more horizontal location before we end up having to call 9-1-1."

"I'm on board with that, but first you'll have to release me from the Jaws of Life. I couldn't move if my life depended on it."

"Oh." She blinked and surveyed the situation. "That's fair, but keep holding me up until I'm sure I won't fall. I can't feel my feet. This is why they invented the innerspring, you know."

"I was headed there, but we ran out of time."

That made her laugh. "True." She eased away from him and lowered her feet to the floor. "I was considering dragging you down into the dirt of the front yard, which I see was a really bad idea now that I'm calmer— but it seemed perfectly logical at the time."

"I would have let you, too, which tells you how

far gone I was. In fact, I'm pretty sure the door to my pickup is still open."

"Probably. I loved that part where you leaped out of the truck. At some point when I hurried out to meet you, I had this awful thought that you wouldn't be as eager to see me as I was to see you, and you'd wonder what the hell I was doing waiting for you in the front yard."

"Instead I was so excited I damned near strangled myself on my seat belt trying to get out of my truck."

She cradled his face in both hands and gazed up at him. "Thank you for meeting me halfway across the yard. It was like something out of a movie."

"It was almost like something out of a Three Stooges movie, but at least neither of us fell down."

Standing on tiptoe, she kissed him gently on the mouth and pulled back. "We need to talk. I found a couple of old camp chairs and put them out on the front porch. Did you notice?"

"Nope. Blew right past those."

"I thought it would be a good place to sit and dis-cuss...things."

He swallowed. Now that the driving need for her had eased, he had time to think about what else they had going on, like the future of this ranch. "Let me duck into your bathroom and get myself sorted out first."

"I thought you'd want to do that. I have coffee, iced tea, beer or wine. Which do you want?"

"Iced tea, please."

"Okay." She started to move away.

He caught her arm. "You're impressing the hell out of me. You've been here, what...less than two days? And yet you're already set up to provide warm hospi-tality to visitors. Last night you made the dining room so nice and tonight you've found another pleasant spot to entertain me. Wow."

She beamed at him. "Now I get to say my line. That's *living with grace*."

He groaned. "I walked right into that one, didn't I?"

"Yep. Perfect setup." She eased away from him and straightened her clothes. "I'll go close the door of your truck. I heard raccoons scrambling around last night and you don't want some critter getting in there."

"Thanks. That would be great."

"Meet you on the porch in a few." She slipped out the front door.

"I'll be there," he called after her. Then he walked through the house to her pink bathroom and took care of business. While drying his hands on her fluffy pink towel, he caught a glimpse of himself in her medicine cabinet mirror. He looked *besotted*.

He'd heard that word once in a high school English class and had always thought it sounded unmanly. No real guy would let himself be described that way, as if some woman had sucked out his brain and replaced it with foam packing peanuts. But that was exactly how the guy in the mirror looked.

He hoped to hell that expression was a result of the amazing sex, and not because he was falling for Bethany. Sex and love weren't the same thing—any reasonable person knew that. Leaning against the counter, which wiggled and was definitely *not* strong enough to have sex on, he peered at himself. Damn, he even seemed *younger*.

He'd become so used to his normal expression that he'd thought nothing of it. But last week he'd been running errands in Shoshone and had stopped at his mom's ice-cream parlor, Lickity Split, to get a cone and see how she was doing. She'd commented on his sad face.

His mother worried about him because he was the family member without a happy ending. Last fall his widowed mom and Ronald Hutchinson, owner of the Shoshone Feed Store, had married. In a cozy little co-incidence, Nash's little sister, Katrina, had become engaged to Ronald's son Langford, known to his close friends, of whom Nash was one, as Hutch.

That left Nash as the lone wolf with no sweetie to warm his bed at night. He hadn't planned it that way, but he hadn't chosen wisely, which explained the sad face his mother had noticed last week. She'd approve of this new expression, but he was better off not showing it to her because at the end of the week, it might disappear.

The clink of ice cubes dropping into glasses told him that Bethany was getting the iced tea ready. For one brief moment he allowed himself to imagine what life would be like if he and Bethany lived in this house together. He liked the idea so much it hurt. Dismissing what was a pointless fantasy, he walked into the kitchen.

She wasn't there, which meant she'd taken the iced tea out to the porch, where they'd agreed to meet. She could have come looking for him, but she hadn't because they didn't know each other that well yet. He didn't miss Lindsay, but he missed the ease with which married couples interacted after living together for years.

He wanted that again with someone, and a couple of kids thrown into the bargain would be okay, too. Being around the Chance family had given him a new yardstick for what made up the good life. For Lindsay, it had meant a luxurious home, expensive vehicles and tropical vacations.

Now that Nash had none of those things, he'd discovered they weren't important to him. Instead he longed for something he'd never had—a loving relationship with a woman who shared his dreams. He wondered if Bethany longed for anything or if she was happy with her life as it was.

Pushing open the screen door, he heard crickets chirping and noticed that a sliver of moon hung in the navy blue sky. A soft breeze brought the familiar scent of sage that he always associated with Jackson Hole.

The light coming through the screen door was just enough to make out two faded canvas chairs on the weathered porch with a wooden stool between them. A tray with one iced tea glass and a plate of brownies topped the stool.

Bethany glanced up from the far chair and smiled at him. She had a tall glass in one hand and his hat on her lap. "Have a seat, cowboy. I retrieved your hat. Didn't know if you wanted it."

"Thank you." He took the hat from her before sitting down, but he hung it over the arm of the chair instead of putting it on.

"You don't want to wear it?" She picked up his iced tea glass and gave it to him.

"Not right now."

"I thought cowboys felt naked without their hats."

He laughed. "Normally that's true, but when I'm around you, I figure it's better to leave it off rather than risk having it knocked off in the midst of whatever we might be doing."

"Mmm." She sipped her tea. "You make me sound wild."

"Not just you. I take my share of responsibility for any wildness that's been going on." And all that wildness had made him thirsty. He took a hefty swallow of tea. "This is great." Then he grabbed a brownie.

"So, Morgan gave me a figure."

He kept eating the brownie, but the taste was gone. "And? How much?"

"I don't know that it matters."

His heart hammered. "You've decided not to sell." He should have guessed she might. Morgan loved this area and might have made a good case for holding on to the property.

"No, I'm going to sell." She glanced at him. "To you."

He froze. "You are?"

"Yes. And I'll tell you why. I can trust you not to tear everything down and start over."

"Who said anything about doing that?"

"Morgan warned me about the possibility. She said, and rightly so, that a buyer might love the land and the view but not the structures. Most of the value is tied up in the land."

His heart continued to pound, but now he was dealing with the adrenaline rush of her announcement that he could buy the Triple G. He struggled to keep his wits about him. "You'll have to tell me what that is. It might be out of my price range."

"It won't be. Whatever you have to put down is fine, and we'll work with the bank on the loan. It's my property, so I could sell it to you for a dollar if I wanted to. That would look weird, though, so we'll work out a deal that you can handle."

He took a deep breath and let it out slowly in an attempt to calm his racing pulse. "I'm not going to let false pride stand in my way, Bethany. I accept your generosity and I'll be eternally grateful for it. I'll buy all your previous books and any future books to prove my gratitude."

"Good grief, don't go overboard! You hate my books."

"No, I don't. Not anymore, at least. At one time I had you labeled as some fluff-brain who didn't know what she was talking about, but now that I know you, I realize that you're really smart and I could probably learn some things from your books."

She stared at him. "So you're actually going to read them?"

"I didn't say that." He grinned at her. "I just said I might learn something if I did. I might learn something if I read *War and Peace,* too, but that doesn't mean I'm gonna do it."

"If I had something to throw at you, I would. Honestly, Nash." But she chuckled, which meant she realized he was teasing her and wasn't mad at him.

"You can throw anything you want. Just don't change your mind about selling me the Triple G."

"I won't. I'll call Morgan first thing in the morning and tell her what I'm up to. She wasn't going to get the listing up until tomorrow anyway."

Nash gazed out at the dark and silent barn…his barn. His tractor barn, too, and his chicken coop. The porch they were sitting on would be his. "I can't believe it. It's not real to me."

"It's not real to me, either." She sighed. "But it's the right thing to do. And I promise you I won't change my mind."

"You're sad."

She glanced over at him. "Not as sad as I would be if someone I didn't know bought this place and bull-dozed it."

"If you care about it so much, why not keep it?" He was an idiot for putting that thought in her mind, but his conscience forced him to.

"I'll be too far away to keep track of it. And too busy. I didn't tell you before, but Opal Knightly has asked me to become a permanent part of her talk show. If that goes well…who knows? I might have my own show someday."

He sat in stunned silence for a moment. Although he wasn't much of a TV watcher, even he knew Opal had a huge following. Everybody loved Opal, and she was one of the richest women in the country. "That's… incredible, Bethany. What an opportunity. No wonder you want to get out from under this ranch."

"Yep. It's all wrong for me, but it's perfect for you."

"It is." He continued to digest the news that she was about to become a TV celebrity on top of her bestselling-author status. If he'd considered her out of reach before, now she was a galaxy away. "What do you want me to do about the repairs?"

"I've thought about that, too. The outbuildings need work, but repairing them wouldn't change the look of the ranch too terribly much. This house, though, has potential. Morgan and I discovered hardwood floors under the old carpet."

"You did?" He struggled to focus on the conversa-tion, but he was still thinking about the Opal bombshell She'd be appearing on TV five days a week. He could tune in and see her there. He wouldn't, but he could.

"Morgan ripped up one little section. Before I leave for Atlanta, I'd like you to help me fix up the house, at least a little bit. I haven't seen it as it could be since I was a little girl, and I'd like that image to take with me."

"Sure. I'd be happy to do that."

She turned to him. "That might mean more work and less sex."

"However you want to play this, Bethany. You've just given me a whole new lease on life. However you want to roll is how we'll do it."

"I'm not saying we won't have *any* sex."

That made him smile. "Good to hear." She might be headed for even greater fame and fortune, but she hadn't left yet, and for some reason, she craved his body. He wasn't going to turn down that kind of opportunity.

He set his iced tea glass on the tray. "So what's your pleasure? We have at least two hours before I have to leave. I'm at your service." He forced himself not to anticipate, to be cool with whatever she asked for.

She stood. "Let me show you the place where Morgan pulled up the carpet."

"Okay." So it would be renovation, then. He was fine with that. He picked up his iced tea. Might as well polish it off before they got started.

"And before I show you the floor…"

He expected her to explain how they'd go about tearing out the carpet.

"Let's boink until we can't see straight."

He spewed his mouthful of tea. This was turning into one hell of a night.

9

BETHANY'S TWIN BED LIMITED how many sexual positions they could reasonably enjoy, and for their second experience, she'd chosen to be the one on top. That had proven most satisfactory. In a postorgasmic daze, she lay slumped against Nash's broad chest, her head nestled on his shoulder.

He slid his hand over the curve of her rump and squeezed. "You have a terrific ass."

"Same to you." She sighed happily. "Yours is very pinch-worthy, in fact."

"Is that so?" He pinched her hard enough to make her squeak in protest. "Fancy that," he said. "Yours is, too."

"No fair. I can't reach you." She tried to slide her hand under him but he seemed welded to the mattress.

Laughing, he grabbed her wrist. "Give it up, Ms. Grace. You shouldn't have planted the idea in my head when your sweet fanny was sticking up in the air so temptingly."

With her free hand, she pushed on his chest until she was straddling him and sitting on the fanny in question, although they remained intimately linked. The firmness of his erection, she'd discovered to her delight, was slow to recede. "A gentleman wouldn't have taken advantage of the situation," she said. "I may have a bruise."

He gave her a smile filled with wicked intent. "I never claimed to be a gentleman. Think of that little bruise as a reminder that I was there."

She probably would, too. "Just know that I'll be gunning for you, Bledsoe. Sometime when you least expect it, I'll return the favor."

"With luck I'll have sunk my cock deep inside you when that happens and I won't mind a bit. But right now, you need to move so I can get up."

She eased away from him and he carefully climbed out without pushing her onto the floor. She recovered her balance and sat cross-legged on the bed. "This space restriction is getting old. We need room to spread out."

"I like the sound of that," he said over his shoulder as he walked into her bathroom. "What are our options?"

She'd been thinking about it earlier as she'd imagined the night's activities and another round of sex in her narrow bed. One answer would be to get rid of the old bed in her parents' room and have a furniture store in Jackson deliver a king-size. But she couldn't very well suggest that now that he would be the home's new owner.

"Here's an idea," he said, walking out of the bathroom. "I'll need a new bed anyway. If you wouldn't object, I could check and see if there's any furniture store in Jackson that could deliver one tomorrow."

"My thought exactly! But it wasn't my suggestion to make."

"So you wouldn't care? We'd have to haul out your parents' old bed."

"The sooner the better. In fact, I think almost all the

furniture needs to go. Just tell me if there's anything you want to keep." The idea of starting fresh excited her.

"The dining room table and chairs, unless you're taking them."

"Nope. Not shipping furniture to Atlanta. At the most, I'll have a couple of boxes of pictures and keepsakes sent there. The dining set is good quality, though, so I'm glad you want it."

He gazed at her. "And that bed."

"*This one?* Why?"

Something in his expression told her exactly why, and she decided not to question him any further and expose his sentimental side. He might not appreciate that. "I suppose it would work for guests."

"Yeah. Always good to have a spare bed. Might as well leave me the sheets, too. Save me from buying some."

Maybe he was simply being practical, but she didn't think so. She hadn't studied psychology for years without learning something about people. He might eventually get rid of both the bed and the sheets when her memory had faded and he'd found someone to love, but for now it represented a significant change in his life and he wanted a reminder.

"Anything else?" she asked. "Want to take a walk-through to refresh your memory?"

"Sure. Let me put something on. I know we're in the middle of the country with no one else around, but I've never been the kind of guy who walks around naked in his house."

She liked that he'd unconsciously mentioned that the house was his. "I'm not the kind of woman who does that, either." She reached for her running shorts and halter top.

"Now, see, I wouldn't mind at all if you wanted to do that." He winked at her as he pulled on his briefs and picked up his jeans.

"Not my style." She slipped into her running shorts. "Besides, I have this theory that if a woman parades around naked all the time, the man in her life will eventually become so used to seeing her without clothes on that it won't arouse him anymore."

"I'd love to test that theory this week." He focused on her bare breasts as he buttoned and zipped his jeans.

"A week might not be long enough."

He glanced away. "No, probably not." His tone was brisk, all the teasing gone.

She fought a wave of sadness. Although she knew their time limit was a blessing in many ways, it was a curse in others. Happiness Is a Choice. Time to put her motto to a very tough test.

While she tied her halter top, he shoved his arms into the sleeves of his shirt but left it unfastened. It was a sexy look on him. Of course, he looked sexy no matter what he had on or didn't have on. The guy couldn't look bad if he tried.

"Let's start with the kitchen." She walked out of the bedroom barefoot and noticed that he did the same, which she found very cute. They were beginning to relax around each other. They were building a relationship whether they meant to or not.

She gestured to the round wooden kitchen table and four chairs. "Do you want that?"

He walked around it, viewing it from all sides. Then he braced both hands on the top and tried to wiggle it.

The table barely moved. "Nice and solid. Just needs some refinishing. I'll keep it."

"Okay." She glanced down at the cracked linoleum. "This needs to come up but I'm more interested in working on the carpeting first."

"Your call."

She stood in the kitchen and thought about everything in the cupboards—her mother's old pots and pans, the silverware her parents had been given as a wedding present, the good china, the crystal glasses. Then there was all the everyday stuff, including inexpensive glasses, regular dishes and stainless flatware.

After living on her own for years, she'd invested in all that for herself. She didn't need any of this, and although it had some sentimental value, she had no extra space in her Atlanta town house. "You can have anything in the cupboards you want," she said.

"You're sure?"

"Yes, unless you don't want any of it."

"Bethany, I have nothing. I'd be happy to have all of it, but I don't know if that's fair to you."

"You'd be saving me a lot of trouble. If I sold to anyone else but you, I'd have to clean out those cupboards."

He nodded. "I see your point, but I still think you're being incredibly generous with your stuff."

"Like I said, you're making life easier for me."

"Okay, then." He smiled at her. "Thank you."

"That means we don't have to deal with anything in here for now, and the dining table stays, so let's check out the living room. I'll show you the little piece of hardwood flooring Morgan uncovered."

Nash followed her through the dining room and into what was her least favorite room in the house. It should have been a family gathering place, but instead it had been dominated by her father's silent unhappiness. She remembered evenings when the television was the only noise in the room.

The furniture reflected that dismal memory. The upholstery was stained and the television set was old and outdated. Even the coffee table was veneer on particle board instead of solid wood.

Crouching down next to the flap of carpet Morgan had created, Bethany pulled hard and more dust flew. It made her sneeze, but she'd exposed a good square foot of wood flooring.

Nash dropped to one knee and brushed away some of the grime. "This will be gorgeous. Definitely oak."

"That's why I'd love to see it finished before I leave." She stood. "So, does anything in here interest you?"

He rose to his feet. "That's a leading question if I ever heard one."

"I meant *furniture,* Bledsoe. Focus."

"Oh, I'm focused." He gave her a long, slow once-over. "Extremely focused."

Her nipples tightened, pushing against the thin material of her red halter top. Warmth tinged her skin as her pulse began to pound.

"Judging from the visual evidence," he murmured, "so are you, sweetheart."

She sucked in a breath. "We're almost finished with the furniture evaluation."

"Slave driver." He gave her a crooked grin.

"I just need to know what you want."

"I think you know exactly what I want." He reached out and rubbed his thumb over her lower lip. "And how I want it."

She was so tempted to lead him right back into that bedroom, but that would end this discussion before she found out what she could get rid of tomorrow. She was impatient to clear the most horrible pieces out of here before he came back.

"Humor me and check out the furniture in here, okay? Then I'm all yours."

"Promise?"

"I cross my heart." She made the age-old sign over her chest.

He smiled. "That's one of my favorite George Strait songs."

"Really?" She vaguely remembered it. "Why?"

"It's about promises, which I happen to believe are very important." He sighed. "That's one of the reasons I had so much trouble giving up on my marriage. I'd promised."

"That's admirable." Emotion clogged her throat. Promises were a loaded subject for her. Her father had been a casual giver of promises that never came true. Here was a man who'd clung to a toxic marriage because he'd given his word.

"Probably stupid, too," he said.

She shook her head. "No. Not stupid. It means you're a guy who can be counted on."

"Thank you." He met her gaze and held it.

In that moment, she had the crazy thought that Nash was the sort of man a girl shouldn't let get away.

Then he broke eye contact. "Okay. Furniture." He swept the room with one glance. "The TV's not worth much, but the couch and chair aren't too bad."

She cleared her throat. "Yes, they are. They've been

here for twenty years, at least, maybe longer. The springs are shot and the upholstery's ruined."

He took another look. "Yeah, but maybe if they were recovered, they could be salvaged."

Without meaning to, she made a little sound of distress.

He studied her. "You want all this out of here, don't you?"

Although she had her mouth open to say "hell, yes," she realized that he was the one who'd be replacing the furniture, not her. If he could get a good deal on reupholstering the couch and chair, he might save money. Maybe he didn't care that the coffee table was cheap veneer.

If she couldn't have all this hauled away tomorrow, tearing out the carpet wouldn't be as easy, but she could still do it by moving the hateful furniture around. "It's up to you, Nash."

His blue eyes twinkled. "You should see your face. It's all kind of pinched in, as if you had to force those words out of your sweet little mouth."

"Hey." She couldn't help smiling because he was absolutely right. "I may despise this furniture and dream of taking a sledgehammer to it, but—"

"Or a can of gasoline and a butane lighter?"

"No, I won't try that again. Furniture doesn't burn the way it used to. I should have used a sledgehammer on that recliner."

"But if you had, we might never have met."

Her gaze locked with his once again. "It seems incredible that we might have missed each other."

"But we didn't because you decided to send me smoke signals."

"Yeah." She had to look away because the intimate warmth reflected in his eyes hinted at feelings neither of them should allow themselves. But she liked basking in that warmth, so she indulged herself a little longer.

"Get rid of the couch and chair." Amusement laced his words. "The cheesy coffee table can go, too."

"Thank you."

"In fact, if you feel a sledgehammer moment coming on, I'll take the chair outside right now so you can whale away on it. Then you'll be all heated up and we can have rip-roaring sex afterward."

"I don't need to destroy anything at the moment. However, I do need the name of somebody who'll haul it away, along with the bed in the master and the dresser in there. It's the same quality as the coffee table, so you don't want it, either."

"When you call Morgan tomorrow you can ask her for a recommendation. She'll know somebody. She deals with this kind of thing all the time."

"Great. Once the furniture's out of here, I can start ripping up the carpet. Maybe by the time you arrive tomorrow night, I'll have it all gone." In fact, she planned on it.

He frowned. "That's a tough, nasty job. I don't want you doing it alone."

"I wouldn't mind at all. In fact, it would be therapeutic."

"Well, you're not the only one who could use some therapy, you know. In fact, my ex seemed to think I needed tons of it. How about leaving the carpet and we'll rip it out together?"

"You'll get filthy and tired."

"So will you. And then we can shower off together."

"I wanted to have it all out of here when you came over."

"And I want you to wait for me. Let's see if I can convince you to do that." Without warning, he scooped her up in his arms.

"Nash! Are you manhandling me?"

"I certainly hope so, since I'm a man and I plan to handle you. A lot." He carried her through the dining room, being careful not to bang her feet against the chairs surrounding the table.

"I told you we could have sex after we decided on the furniture. You don't have to abduct me."

"Yes, I do. It's more fun this way."

She had to admit it was damned thrilling to be carried off to bed like Scarlett O'Hara, except he wasn't aiming for her bedroom. Instead, he kicked two of the kitchen chairs aside and sat her on the wooden table.

She glanced up at him as his obvious intent dawned on her. "Are you really—"

"Yes." He grabbed her running shorts by the elastic. "Lift up."

"I don't know about this. What if the table breaks?"

"It won't. That's why I tested it earlier. Lift up."

"You planned on this?"

"You talk too much." Leaning down, he kissed her while he began pulling her shorts off. As his tongue worked its magic, she became more compliant. Bracing her weight on her arms, she raised her hips, and soon her shorts were on the floor and her bare bottom was resting on the table's smooth coolness.

He straightened, his breathing labored. "Now take your top off." He pulled another condom from his pocket and held it in his teeth while he unfastened his jeans.

"Bossy, aren't we?" But she did as she was told.

He took the condom packet from between his teeth and ripped it open. "Sorry. When I'm agitated, I give orders."

"And I agitate you?"

"Aw, honey, you have no idea." Reaching down, he grasped her ankles. "Brace yourself on your arms again. This is the fun part."

She gasped as he lifted her legs and hooked her heels over his shoulders. "Nash!" She'd never felt so open and exposed in her life.

"Easy does it, sweetheart. You'll be fine." Palms flat on the table on either side of her hips, he probed her moist center with the head of his penis. "Ah, there you are." And he thrust deep, nearly lifting her off the table.

She gasped again. He filled her to the brim and touched her in places she could swear no man had ever gone before. The sensation of having him so deep inside her, and being unable to move at all, was...incredible. She almost felt as if she could come without him doing a single other thing. Almost.

He leaned forward, his gaze searching hers. "How're you doing, sweetheart?"

She nodded, not sure she could form actual words. But she loved looking into his eyes, which burned with the same fire that licked through her veins.

"Good?"

She nodded again.

"Your pupils are huge. I think you're liking this. I'm glad. I won't last long at this angle."

She managed a strained response. "Me, either."

"Let's see." Holding her gaze, he eased back and pushed forward again. "Ah, I felt you grab me."

"Mmm." She strained toward the climax dangling just out of reach.

He paused and leaned forward again, his mouth hovering over hers. "Promise me something."

She swallowed. "Anything. I need…"

"This?" He stroked her again very slowly.

Almost there. "Yes. More."

"Promise not to rip out the carpet yourself."

Carpet? He was talking about carpet at a time like this? "*Nash.* For the love of—"

"Promise me." He shoved in tight again and held them both perfectly motionless.

She ached for more of that sweet friction. It wouldn't take much.

"Promise." He withdrew again with exquisite slowness.

She'd lost track of the conversation in the blast furnace of her lust. "Promise what?"

"The carpet."

"Yes! Whatever! Now do me!"

"You bet, sweetheart. You bet." And he began to pump into her with a speed that made her body clench tighter, and tighter, and…with a cry, she hurtled into the whirlpool of her climax. He followed her there, his body shuddering as he gasped out her name.

Her arms began to shake as her climax ebbed, leaving her flooded with pleasure. Murmuring words of gratitude, he gently disentangled their bodies and carried her to the bed, where he covered her up.

As she drifted between wakefulness and sleep, she was vaguely aware that he'd gone into the bathroom, and later on he'd picked up his boots from the floor.

Last of all, she felt his lips brush her cheek. "Don't rip out the carpet without me," he said softly.

"'Kay," she murmured in response, and smiled sleepily. He wouldn't have had to work so hard to secure her agreement, but she wouldn't tell him that. His wild performance had been fun.

"I'll lock the door behind me."

"Mmm."

"Wish I could stay." And then he was gone, walking through the house and turning out lights as he went. The front door opened and closed, and soon afterward his truck rumbled to life.

Wish I could stay. Her eyes snapped open as she registered his tone. Tender, longing, *loving.* He was falling for her. That realization was bad enough. But even worse than that, from her standpoint, was that she was falling for him.

10

EDDIE AND ACE SEEMED to have become Nash's charges. Emmett had sent all three of them on a short ride first thing in the morning, and Nash had managed to bring them back alive. Considering how green they were, he thought that was a major accomplishment. He was teaching them how to unsaddle the horses when Sarah walked over from the house.

A tall woman whose blond hair had gone white, she carried herself with the same regal bearing as her mother, who had been a runway model in New York. Her clear blue eyes missed nothing. Because she and his mother, Lucy, were best friends, Nash had always considered Sarah kin.

Her smile encompassed both the boys and Nash. "Congratulations on a successful outing."

Eddie and Ace stood there in awkward silence. They'd chattered away during the entire ride, but Miss Sarah, as they called her, obviously intimidated them. Nash thought that was a good thing. Sarah deserved their utmost respect, as she also deserved his.

"They did great," Nash said, filling the silence. "Born

riders, both of them." He was stretching the truth a little, but the kids needed confidence.

"I thought they would be from the minute I met them." Sarah glanced at Nash. "When you're finished here, I'd like to see you up at the house."

"I can be there in ten minutes."

"Terrific. See you then. Pay attention to Nash, boys. He knows what he's doing."

They both mumbled, "Yes, ma'am," and stared at the ground. But once she'd left, they each had plenty to say.

Ace led off. "You are in *trou*-ble." He wagged his head knowingly. "She's calling you up there to give you a talking-to."

"Yeah, she is," Eddie piped in. "A boss lady like that doesn't come down here looking for someone unless she wants to give you what for." The boy looked worried. "I hope she's not going to fire you."

Nash chuckled. "She's not. I haven't given her any reason to do that."

"Maybe it's something you don't even know you did!" Ace was getting into the spirit of this new development. "Sometimes my foster dad gets all upset when I didn't do *anything.* So then I'm all like, 'what'd I do?' And he's all like, 'you know perfectly well what you did.' But I don't."

Nash's heart ached for the kid, who'd never known unconditional love and had to work within a system that didn't often provide it. "Sarah doesn't look for things to gripe about. And you notice she was smiling when she came down here. If she had a problem with me, she wouldn't cover it up with smiles. She's not like that."

"That's good." Eddie nodded. "My stepmom can be smiling one minute and smack you the next. You never know what'll happen. That's why I like it here. You know what to expect."

"Yeah." Ace laughed. "You can expect them to work you to death."

Nash raised his eyebrows. "Excuse me?"

"Okay, maybe not *to death*. That would be child abuse. But we work hard."

"So do I," Nash said quietly. "And I'm grateful for a roof over my head and three meals a day."

Ace rolled his eyes. "Oh, man, the Chances sure brainwashed you!"

Eddie punched him in the arm. "Knock it off. You like it here, and they don't work us *that* hard. Like tonight we get to watch a movie under the stars. We're gonna have popcorn and everything. I don't know about you, but I think that's cool."

"It's okay." Ace wasn't ready to drop his mask of indifference just yet.

Nash looked forward to the day he did. He thought it would come before Ace left the ranch in the middle of August. For now, he was protecting himself, and Nash certainly understood that impulse.

After the boys had returned the saddles, blankets and bridles where they belonged and had used a currycomb on their horses, Nash released them to Emily, Emmett's daughter. She was in training to take over as foreman someday, and Emmett was proud as punch about that.

The boys worked harder for Emily than anyone else because they thought she was hot. Nash had heard them bemoaning the fact that she was married. Today she'd set up a fence-mending operation, and although the kids might think of themselves as unpaid labor, the jobs they were doing would take twice as long because they had to learn the basics first.

Nash had gone from dreading the presence of the kids to active interest in their progress. Until he'd worked with them, he'd viewed their arrival as a nuisance. The ranch ran smoothly without this interruption, so why introduce it?

But now he was a fan. He'd been lucky enough to grow up in a loving family, but not everyone got that kind of break. Pete Beckett had identified a need in the community, and hooking up with the Last Chance had been a no-brainer. The love that had developed between Sarah and Pete only added to the beauty of the plan.

Feeling proud to be a part of the Last Chance and all it stood for, Nash walked up to the main house to find out what Sarah had on her mind. Because he'd been hanging around this ranch for years, he sometimes took it for granted, but as he approached the two-story log house, he saw it as the eight kids might.

It was immense. A center section had been the first structure built when the grandparents, both deceased now, had settled here. As the family had grown to include their son, and later their three grandsons, they'd added two wings that were cantilevered out like arms reaching to embrace visitors.

The generous square footage was perfect for the new youth program because the extra bedrooms upstairs could be used as dormitory-style quarters. Two sets of bunks had been constructed in adjoining rooms to accommodate the kids. No matter how jaded Ace pretended to be, he had to feel deep down that he'd died and gone to heaven.

A wide front porch ran the length of the house, and

it was lined with rockers. Sarah occupied one, and she held a mug of coffee in her hand. A second mug sat on the small table between her and an adjoining rocker.

As Nash mounted the steps, he couldn't help thinking of Bethany's more modest arrangement over at the Triple G. But she had the same gift as Sarah: an instinct for how to provide a relaxed atmosphere where two people could have a quiet conversation.

"Come join me," Sarah said. "If I remember correctly, you take yours black."

"I do, and thanks, Sarah." He touched the brim of his hat in greeting. As a kid he'd called her Mrs. Chance, but somewhere along the line, after he'd passed thirty, she'd asked him to use her first name. He settled into the rocker and picked up his coffee.

She cradled her mug in both hands and looked at him. "I heard you're likely to become our new neighbor, so I thought I'd confirm the news at the source."

He'd figured that was why she'd called him up to the house. He should have expected Morgan to mention it to her husband, Gabe, who would have told Sarah. That was how things went around here, and Nash didn't care. He knew they were all happy for him, and that was a good feeling.

"Apparently so," he said. "Bethany thinks that will be easier than going through the listing process, and I'm not about to argue with her about that."

Sarah laughed. "I should hope not. I was tickled to hear it. I know you want your own place, and I'm thrilled when one of my boys gets what he wants out of life."

He loved being referred to as one of *her boys*. His mother might bristle at that, but she'd realized long ago that Sarah had swept him into her family net. "It's like a dream come true," he said. "She's willing to be flexible with the financing, and her original plan to renovate the Triple G isn't so important now. I can work on it in my spare time." He took a sip from his mug. The coffee, as always, was primo. Mary Lou, the Last Chance cook, saw to that.

"I don't want to pry into your personal business, but if you need any financial backing to close the deal, just say the word. I've discussed it with Jack and we'll be happy to cosign or loan you what you need."

"Thanks, Sarah." He gazed at her and thought what a lucky guy he was to have friends like these. "I hope I won't need that, but I appreciate the offer."

"Just keep it in mind." Sarah beamed at him. "Have you told your mother?"

"Uh, no." He realized that he probably should get on that ASAP. Maybe he was already too late. "Have you?"

"No, dear boy. I wouldn't do that to you. But if you don't tell her soon, she'll find out from someone else, and then you'll have hell to pay."

"Good point."

"I have a few things I need in town. Why don't you take care of those errands for me and drop by the ice-cream parlor while you're there?"

"Be happy to." But his mind was racing. He didn't want to confront his mother while he was involved with Bethany. Eagle-eyed Sarah had probably noticed a difference in him, but she wouldn't think it was her place to ask questions. His mother, who liked to remind him she was the one who'd brought him into the world, would consider it her God-given right to interrogate him.

Sarah rose from her chair. "Come on inside. I'll get my list. Bring your coffee. Mary Lou might have a few things she wants to add."

Nash couldn't shake the feeling that his personal relationship with Bethany, which he'd hoped to keep private, was about to become public. And it wasn't only his privacy he was worried about. Bethany wanted to remain anonymous this week. Being romantically linked with him wouldn't help her cause any.

Sarah led the way through the rustic yet elegant living room with its giant stone fireplace, sturdy leather furniture and Native American rugs hanging on the walls. A curved staircase built by Archie Chance rose to the second story, and a wagon-wheel chandelier hung from the ceiling.

The Triple G would never look like this because it hadn't been built on the same grand scale. But Nash decided then and there that he'd put in a rock fireplace. Smaller, of course, but maybe that living room would no longer seem drab and soulless if it had a fireplace.

He'd change that and bring new life to the house with a cozy hearth and a blazing fire. He wished that Bethany would be able to see it, but she'd be long gone by the time he finished. He wondered if she'd want him to text a picture. Maybe not. Maybe she'd prefer they have no contact once she left Jackson Hole.

That was a depressing thought, so he pushed it out of his mind. If he walked into Mary Lou's kitchen looking sad, she'd try to feed him. Much as he loved her food, he didn't want to waste time hanging around the ranch kitchen when he should be making tracks for his mother's ice-cream parlor.

He smelled lunch cooking as they walked down the

long hallway that led to the good-sized dining room where the hands ate lunch every day. Breakfast and supper were prepared and eaten at the bunkhouse, but the Chance family believed in gathering the whole crew together for lunch.

Nash gave a lot of credit to that tradition and Mary Lou's down-home meals for creating such loyalty among the hands. Mary Lou Sims had been in charge of the Last Chance kitchen for as long as Nash could remember. An independent woman in her mid-fifties, she'd remained stubbornly single until last summer, when she'd finally married the ranch hand everyone knew by his last name, Watkins. She'd kept her own last name, insisting she preferred the sound of it.

When Sarah and Nash entered the fragrant kitchen, Mary Lou had both ovens and three burners going. She moved quickly around the space with the precision developed over a thirty-year career. When she'd checked everything to make sure all was well, she turned to them with a smile, her wispy gray hair sticking out in all directions. "What's up?"

"Nash is going into town and I wondered if you needed anything," Sarah said.

"I expect you'll be going by the Lickity Split," Mary Lou said, "so you can tell your mother about buying the Triple G."

"Yes, ma'am, I will." Nash felt like an eight-year-old being reminded of his chores. Only a few people could take that tone with him. Mary Lou was one and his mom was another.

"Then while you're there, I'd like you to pick up three gallons of chocolate peanut butter swirl. I'm letting the boys have ice cream tonight, besides the popcorn. They don't know that yet, so don't tell them."

Nash grinned. "I won't. But that's a nice touch. I thought Pete's idea of setting up a screen and projector outside was brilliant. But adding in chocolate peanut butter swirl is even more brilliant. That might wipe the sulky expression off Ace's mug, at least for a little while." He almost wished he'd be there to see it, but he had a date with a carpet and a hot woman.

"That was part of my devious plan. I'm gunning for that Ace kid." Mary Lou glanced over at Sarah. "Did you mention tomorrow night yet?"

"Not yet." Sarah turned to Nash. "Morgan says Bethany's very nice, and I have to agree with that assessment if she's willing to work with you on financing that ranch. We've been remiss in not doing this sooner, but I'd like to invite her to dinner tomorrow night. It's the neighborly thing to do."

Nash tried not to panic. It was only dinner. No big deal. Except he didn't believe that for a minute. He should have seen this coming. Everyone on this ranch was dying of curiosity as to why he'd suddenly gone from Bethany's handyman to the guy being offered the ranch on a silver platter. Knowing him as he'd been in the old days, they'd all jumped to the same conclusion.

It wasn't the right conclusion, though, he told himself. He hadn't seduced Bethany in order to sweet-talk her into selling him the ranch. She'd done the seducing. He'd even been afraid that having sex with her had ruined his opportunity to buy the ranch.

Fortunately it hadn't, and she wasn't offering it to him because they had fun in bed. At least he hoped to hell that wasn't the reason. She'd told him that she didn't want to risk selling it to someone who'd tear it down. That was her story and he was sticking to it.

Sarah peered at him. "Nash, is anything wrong? You look as if you're in pain. Do you have a stomachache?"

"No, no." He quickly ran a hand over his face. "I'm fun...I mean fine. I'll ask Bethany about dinner. I'm sure she'd love it."

"Good." Sarah continued to study him with a worried look in her blue eyes. "The Grace family has always concerned me, but the parents weren't particularly social, especially the father, so I gave up trying to establish a friendship. Jack doesn't remember Bethany at all from school but she was much younger than you two boys. Gabe and Nick say she kept to herself. But she's doing you a good turn, Nash, so I'd like to thank her for that."

"And I know she'll appreciate it." Nash decided to skedaddle before he put his foot in his mouth. "Anything else you need from town, Mary Lou?"

"Just the ice cream. Hang on a minute. I'll get you a cooler and a couple of ice packs so it'll keep on the way home." She hurried into a large pantry.

Sarah continued to watch him. "You're not upset about this dinner, are you, Nash? I don't have to do it. I just thought—"

"It's a great idea, Sarah. Thank you for coming up with it." He wasn't about to throw her hospitality back in her face. He knew Bethany wouldn't do that, either. But it could be a tense evening as he worried about advertising their close relationship and she worried about being recognized as a bestselling author.

"Okay, then. As long as you're fine with it, you might

as well invite your mother and Ronald while you're in town. They'll want to come."

Nash felt his chest tighten. So everyone wanted to get a look at Bethany, the poor woman. "Sure." He tried to make his response light and breezy. "I'll be happy to invite them."

"We'll have a good time."

"I'm sure we will." He gave Sarah an encouraging smile despite the dread rolling in his stomach.

Moments later, armed with the cooler and a couple of ice packs, he left the house and was soon driving one of the ranch trucks down the bumpy road to the main highway. He never could have imagined that investigating a column of smoke rising in the blue Wyoming sky would lead to all this commotion. But ending up with a ranch of his own was worth any angst he felt now.

Less than fifteen minutes later, he cruised into the little town of Shoshone, which still had only one stoplight at its lone intersection. He glanced around at the small collection of businesses with a new sense of belonging. Soon he'd be a man with a ranch, a man who could buy livestock and a man who could sit on his front porch in the evenings and enjoy a cool one.

That made him so happy he nearly ran the red light. Screeching to a stop, he looked across the intersection to the Spirits and Spurs, the bar that Jack's wife, Josie, owned. Josie insisted the historic bar was haunted by the ghosts of cowboys who used to hang out there. She called them Ghost Drinkers in the Bar. Sometimes she could be coaxed into singing a rendition of "Ghost Riders in the Sky" with the lyrics changed.

Nash decided that after he closed on the Triple G, he'd invite all his friends to the Spirits and Spurs for a celebration. He might even ask Jack to drive him there. He'd be quite likely to tie one on after he became the proud owner of a ranch.

His list of errands was trickier than he'd thought. He'd have to get the ice cream last, which dictated going to the feed store first. That meant talking to his new stepfather, Ronald Hutchinson, without giving anything away, because if he did, Ronald would be on the phone to his new wife over at Lickity Split before Nash could get there.

So he shopped quickly, smiled a lot and said very little to Ronald. Then he drove straight to the ice-cream parlor.

When he walked in, his redheaded mother grinned at him. "Knew you were coming." She walked around the counter and gave him a hug. "Ronald said you were at the feed store and you seemed to be in a powerful hurry."

"That's because I have to tell you something before you hear it from anyone else, and that's a real challenge in this town."

Her eyes widened. "You're engaged to that Grace woman!"

"No! Good Lord, no. Why would you think that?"

"Well, everyone in town is speculating about you two. They say she's real cute, and she's single. You're also very cute and single, and you're working out at her place, and neither of you is getting any younger."

He sighed. "That's true. I've aged several years in the past two minutes." He scowled at her. "Mom, for crying out loud. I wouldn't get engaged to someone I'd known for a few days. I don't care if she's the cutest thing I've ever seen, I still—"

"Is she?"

"Is she what?"

"The cutest thing you've ever seen?"

"Well...uh..."

"I knew it! Your eyes are sparkling like they haven't sparkled in a long time, and that Grace woman is the only change I know of in your life, so I figure she's the reason."

He took her by the shoulders. "I'll tell you the reason, and it's not because I've fallen for the Grace woman—I mean, Bethany. It's because she's agreed to sell me her ranch. I'm going to have my own place!"

"Good!" His mother reached up and pinched his cheeks. "Good for you. Are you and the Grace woman going to live there together? I don't mind if you want to do that. It wasn't right for Ronald and me. I felt we had to get married, but—"

"We won't be living there together." Nash wished he'd said that without a catch in his voice, but maybe she'd missed it.

"Oh, I'm sorry." No, she hadn't missed it.

"Look, I like Bethany, but she's returning to Atlanta at the end of the week. That's where she works."

His mother looked smug. "For now."

"She's not coming back here, Mom. She has an important job in Atlanta and she's staying there."

"Then she's stupid."

"No, she certainly is *not*. And if you're going to take that attitude toward her, then I don't know if you should come to dinner at the Last Chance tomorrow night."

His mother clasped her hands together. "Sarah's having a dinner? Bless that woman. Of course Ronald and I will be there. I'm just sorry your sister and Hutch aren't in town so they can get a look at this Grace woman."

"Her name is Bethany."

"I'll be sure and call her that, too, unless she goes by Beth. Some Bethanys shorten their name to Beth, so maybe I should ask her."

"It's Bethany. She doesn't shorten it."

"So you say the whole blessed thing, too? I would think when you two get cozy, you'd want to shorten it up some."

Nash could think of no way to tackle that comment so he remained in his own silent hell and wondered how he'd ever make it through tomorrow night's dinner.

"I mean, when Ronald and I are getting lovey-dovey, I call him Ron, and he calls me...well, never mind what he calls me."

"I'm glad you spared me that, Mom. Okay, I need three gallons of chocolate peanut butter swirl, and then I have to get back."

"Of course you do. But Bethany must really like ice cream if she's going to eat all that in less than a week."

"It's not for her. Mary Lou's serving it to the boys tonight."

"Oh, well, then what kind of ice cream does Bethany like? You should take her some when you see her tonight."

"Mom!"

"It was just a suggestion. If I were Bethany I'd want you to bring me some of your mother's excellent ice cream."

He folded his arms and stared at her.

"All right, all right. Come back to the freezer and I'll load you up with the chocolate peanut butter swirl."

He didn't get away with just that, of course. It was easier to accept a free pint of fudge ripple for Bethany than argue about it. Yep, tomorrow night would be a real rodeo. Fortunately, he had one more night alone with Bethany before his friends and family blew the lid off their private little affair.

11

THANKS TO MORGAN'S CONTACTS, two burly cowboys had arrived at ten in the morning and had carted away every stick of furniture from both the living room and Bethany's parents' bedroom. A couple of hours prior to that, Bethany had boxed up all the clothes from the master bedroom closet and the rickety dresser. The two men had taken those boxes, too.

That had left her with two empty rooms and the itch to rip up carpeting, but she'd promised not to. She hadn't promised not to rip up the kitchen linoleum, however. Of the two jobs, it had to be the easier one. The glue had dried years ago and the linoleum gave little resistance as she broke it off in chunks and carried it to a trash bin on the little stoop outside the kitchen door.

This floor looked like pine instead of oak, but Bethany thought that might work well for a kitchen that would take some wear and tear. She'd recommend to Nash that he distress the pine so any future scratches and marks blended right in. Anything was better than the ghastly green-and-white-marbled linoleum that someone, probably her dad, had put down.

During one of her trips to the back stoop, she paused to admire the view of the Tetons. As a kid she'd sat out there quite a bit. Her mother had talked about enlarging the stoop into a porch because the view was so spectacular, but Bethany's dad hadn't worked up any enthusiasm for it, so the project had been scrapped.

Even though taking up the linoleum wasn't particularly hard work, the job consumed most of the day. After showering and putting on clean shorts and another halter top, she brought a light supper of chicken salad and a glass of wine outside so she could watch the light changing on the jagged mountains.

She was still there when she heard Nash's truck on the road. He was a little early, but that was fine with her. She could hardly wait to see him and show him the empty rooms.

Carrying her plate and wineglass inside, she set them on the counter as his boots hit the front porch.

"Bethany?" He opened the screen door. "So help me, if you're ripping out that carpet, I'll—"

"You'll what?" She walked through the dining room doorway, hands on hips. Once again he'd left his hat in the truck. But he was still her fantasy cowboy, looking yummy as ever, and he'd arrived bearing gifts. He was holding something in a white paper bag.

"Doesn't matter." He glanced around. "You didn't do it."

"No, because I promised I wouldn't. You're not the only one who values a promise, cowboy."

He gave her a sheepish smile. "Sorry I doubted you, sweetheart."

"But what if I had ripped it out?" She was curious about his reaction. "What would you have done?"

"I dunno. Maybe I'd pin you down and tickle you. That's about as nasty as I get. Then I might have given you a massage, because you'd be sore as hell after doing all that."

"Ooh, a massage. Now there's a consequence I'm interested in." She walked toward him. "Are you good at massages?"

He gathered her into his arms and whatever was in the bag bumped against her fanny. "I've been told so. Take off your clothes and I'll give you a demonstration."

"Not yet." She wrapped both arms around his neck and leaned into his solid warmth. Whatever was in the bag was cold. She'd guess it was ice cream from his mother's shop. "Let's rip up the carpet first."

"I hope that's a euphemism for crazed jungle sex."

"'Fraid not, Tarzan." She rubbed against his growing erection. "You're going to have to tame that bad boy until all this carpet is out the door."

"You're not helping." He cupped her bottom with one large hand and brought her in tight. "If you don't want to end up on your back in the next ten seconds, you'd better stop rubbing your sweet body against my cock."

Her breathing quickened. "You tempt me more than you know, cowboy."

"Good. Invite me back to your bedroom and I'll tempt you some more."

"Gonna smear ice cream all over me?"

"What an excellent suggestion. And here I thought bringing you ice cream was a dumb idea. Just don't tell my mother what we did with it."

"I doubt I'll have the chance, since I wasn't planning on meeting her."

His blue eyes lost their teasing light. "Um…I think you will be meeting her."

"I will?" Bethany had a moment of panic. "She's not out in your truck, is she?"

"No, she's not. Take it easy."

"Whew. For a minute there, I wondered if she'd insisted on coming out to see this ranch you were buying."

"No, she wouldn't interfere like that. But…Sarah's organized a dinner party for tomorrow night, as a thank-you for…for deciding to sell me the ranch."

Bethany stared at him in disbelief. "To thank me? She doesn't have to do that. I told you that this is as much for my benefit as yours. It's a win-win situation."

"I know, but Sarah thinks of me as an adopted son, and she knows how much I've wanted my own place. Getting this ranch, which is right next to the Last Chance, means we'll be neighbors, and she's very happy about that. And grateful."

"I see." Bethany had grown up here and she knew as well as anybody that the Chance family was royalty in this area. An invitation from Sarah Chance was an honor, one not to be taken lightly or, heaven forbid, refused. But it made her uneasy to think of socializing when she didn't want to be recognized.

She could tell Nash wasn't any more comfortable about the invitation than she was. "Who will be there?"

"Sarah and her fiancé, Pete Beckett, the one who dreamed up the youth program, and—"

"That's a plus. I'd like to find out more about that. He sounds like a cool guy, somebody I could invite on my talk show." Then she remembered nobody was supposed to find out about that, or her books. "But I can't mention my career. I'll have to watch what I say."

Nash sighed. "Yeah. That's the dicey part."

The cold carton was beginning to numb her fanny. "Let's put the ice cream away and we can plan our strategy while we rip out carpet."

"Okay." He let her go and followed her into the kitchen. "I knew this dinner thing was going to be a buzz kill. I'm sorry about— Hey! What the hell? You took out the linoleum!"

She opened the freezer door and held out her hand for the bag. "I did." She couldn't resist a smile of triumph. "I only promised not to touch the carpet."

He gave her the ice cream. "Remind me to be more specific the next time I extract a promise from you under duress."

"I enjoyed the duress."

"Me, too, but if we keep talking about it, especially in sight of the kitchen table, we'll never get the carpet out of here." He crouched down and studied the newly revealed floor. "It looks great, Bethany. Thanks." He stood. "But you should have waited for me."

"I couldn't stand it. The house is starting to come alive, and I had to do *something* major to help it along. I had fun, if you must know. I've always hated that linoleum. Getting rid of it made me happy."

He laughed. "And happiness is a choice."

"Exactly! I chose to tear out that effing linoleum to bring myself a boatload of happiness. In fact, I was positively orgasmic after it was gone." She winked at him. "Imagine how I'll feel after we finish with the carpet."

"Wiped out is how you'll feel. I'll be lucky if I get a good-night kiss before you're unconscious."

"That reminds me." She opened a kitchen drawer and pulled out a spare house key attached to a souvenir Yellowstone National Park key ring. It had been the one and only family vacation they'd ever taken. "You should have this."

"You're sure? I'm not legally the owner yet."

"I know, but you're as good as legal. This way when you leave tonight, if I'm as unconscious as you expect me to be, you can lock the regular lock and the dead bolt, too."

"Excellent thought." He tucked the key in his pocket. "I did think of that last night, but fortunately the crime rate's minimal around here. Still, I like the idea of locking you up good and tight."

"That sounded almost medieval. Are you a possessive man, Nash?"

He gazed at her with those clear blue eyes. "When I have the right to be, yes, I am. But I have no rights where you're concerned. That doesn't mean I'm not concerned about your safety, though. Thanks for the key."

The sheer maleness of that statement sent a delicious shiver through her. She remembered when he'd almost called her *his woman*. She didn't approve of that kind of talk, but that didn't mean it didn't get her hot. She blamed that on her cave-dwelling ancestors.

"So." He sent her a challenging glance. "Ready to rip some carpet?"

"You know I am. I even unearthed another X-Acto knife." After taking them out of a drawer, she handed one to him and started into the dining room. "I've been ready to slash that carpet ever since the guys who loaded up the furniture pulled out of the yard."

"I notice they didn't take the recliner, though."

"They offered. Said they'd throw it in the dump for me. I wasn't ready to part with it." She hadn't sorted out her emotions about the recliner yet. It represented both her first meeting with Nash and her troubled relationship with her dad. And her feelings about her dad were more complicated than she'd thought.

"When you are ready to ditch it, let me know and it'll be gone." He surveyed the shadowy living room. "How are we going to see what we're doing?"

"Cover your eyes. There's the ugliest overhead light in the world about to come on. It needs to be replaced with something more lovely, but for this job, it's perfect." She flicked a switch.

"Damn." He blinked in the harsh light. "We could perform surgery in here."

"We will." She swept a hand over the stained carpet, which looked even worse in the overhead light with no furniture to distract the eye. "There's our patient."

"Our patient is terminal."

"Then let's pull the plug." Dropping to her knees next to the spot where Morgan had started the process, she began to cut. "And we need to talk about this dinner."

"Yeah?" He'd chosen to work on the far side of the room, which was probably a wise decision since they couldn't seem to keep their hands off each other when they were within touching distance.

"You hinted that I might be meeting your mother. Will she be there?" Bethany hoped to hell not. She didn't want to meet the mother of the guy she'd been boinking for fun with no thought of a commitment. In her experience, mothers took a dim view of such arrangements.

"She wouldn't miss it."

Bethany groaned. "She's going to give me the third degree, isn't she?"

"Well, she did wonder how an intelligent woman could leave a great catch like me in favor of a career in Atlanta, but you have to remember she's my mother. She thinks I hung the moon, the stars and all the planets."

Bethany was glad she was ripping up carpet because it helped relieve her growing anxiety. "I assume you didn't tell her what I do in Atlanta."

"No, but to be fair, that might have helped her understand. She's picturing you in some boring corporate job and can't imagine why you'd prefer that when you could have a wonderful life in Jackson Hole and amazing sex with me."

"She *said* that?"

"Not in so many words. But she's not some little old lady who blushes at the mention of sex, and she's fully convinced that we're getting it on. She wondered if I called you Beth in our more intimate moments."

"Dear God." Bethany pulled up a large chunk of carpet and coughed as the dust flew. "If she knows I'm going back to Atlanta at the end of the week, she probably thinks I'll take whatever I want from her only son and leave him to sing the blues. She isn't going to like me all that much." She went to work with the knife again.

He talked over the noise of ripping carpet. "I'll let her know I'm fine with you leaving. We've had plenty of examples around here of women who thought they'd be happy in Jackson Hole and discovered too late that they hated it."

"So my story is that I'm not a country girl. I guess that works."

"It should. Like I said, she's my mom, so she doesn't want me to get hurt. She's also more protective since the divorce. I think if she believed she wouldn't get caught, she'd put out a contract on Lindsay."

"Nash!" She sat down on the carpet and swiveled to face the side of the room where he was working. "You do realize you're scaring me to death, right? You're painting a picture of a woman who will feed me to the fishes if she thinks I'm going to hurt you in any way."

"Nah, she's not that scary. Besides, she doesn't want to go to jail."

"Now you're messing with me."

"A little." He glanced over his shoulder. "She's just your average mom. Most of them are like that when it comes to their kids."

"Mine wasn't." After she'd said it, she wished she hadn't. Her mom had been the more cheerful of her parents, but she'd possessed zero backbone when it had come to protecting Bethany from anything, whether it was mean kids at school or her father's constant criticism. But she didn't want to be the object of Nash's pity for that. "Which was fine, by the way," she said. "It only made me stronger."

He put down his knife, got up and came over to her. "I can see that." He sat cross-legged in front of her on the carpet. "A case could be made that if my mom hadn't been so protective, I would have been strong enough to tell Lindsay to go to hell much sooner. But you're the psychologist. You tell me."

She drew her knees up to her chest and wrapped her arms around them. "I think it's always great when a parent stands up for a kid, because then you know that you're worth fighting for."

He nodded. "I did feel that way when my mom stood up for me. I still do."

She envied him, plain and simple. He'd had the childhood she'd wanted. "Nash, I hope you don't blame yourself for marrying Lindsay. You were young and believed love would solve everything."

He met her gaze. "Yeah, I did. Now I know different."

"So it was a lesson learned. It doesn't have to be anybody's fault. You're a great guy, and I hope you find the woman you deserve next time around. She'll be very lucky." For some ridiculous reason her throat tightened as she said that.

"You're great, too." He reached over and closed his hand over hers in a gesture that was all about comfort, not sex. "Some guy will be lucky to have you."

She sniffed. "Thank you."

"I won't let my mom be mean to you." He squeezed her hand. "I'll stick up for you, Bethany. I promise."

"There you go with the promises. You'd better cut that out or you're gonna make me cry." She swiped at her eyes with the back of her free hand. Too late she discovered it was covered in grit, which was now in her eyes. They stung like crazy as she blinked, trying to clear them. "Damn. That was a dumb move."

"Come on into the kitchen." He pulled her to her feet and kept hold of her hand. "A wet towel will get that junk out of your eyes." He laughed as he led her through the dining room. "Some help I am, huh? I come over to make you feel better and now you're blinded by carpet grit."

"I'm the moron who rubbed it into my eyes." And she wasn't sorry, because being taken care of by Nash was a lovely feeling. Standing patiently at the kitchen sink, her face lifted, she opened and closed her eyes on command as he used the corner of a damp towel to flick tiny pieces of dirt out of her eyes.

"There. How does that feel?"

She blinked several times. "Much better. Thank you."

"Can't have my carpet-removing partner out of action." He leaned down and kissed her gently. Then he lifted his head, and desire flickered in his eyes. "That felt way too good, sweetheart. We need to get back in the living room and move to our respective corners immediately."

"Yes, sir. Can I take a rain check on whatever it is you're thinking right now?"

"Yes, ma'am, you may. And I'll give you a hint. It involves ice cream."

"Mmm. And lots of licking?"

"Oh, yeah. Smearing and licking. Licking and smearing."

Lust rocketed through her. "In that case, we should transfer it from the freezer to the refrigerator. That freezer keeps things hard as a rock."

He groaned. "Which pretty much describes me right now. You go ahead into the living room and start ripping out carpet. I desperately want to grab you, and I'm less likely to grab a woman who has a knife in her hand."

"Okay." Smiling, she turned and walked toward the kitchen door. "Don't forget to take the ice cream out."

"I won't. But be warned. Once I come back in there, don't mess with me, because I'll be a lean, mean, carpet-ripping machine."

She glanced back at him. "Will that include taking off your shirt and getting all manly and sweaty?"

"Would you like that?"

"Hell, yeah."

He grinned at her. "Then prepare yourself for the *Nash Bledsoe Show*."

She ran a tongue over her lips and gave him her best sultry gaze. "Bring it on, big boy."

His laughter followed her all the way into the living room. God, but he was a hoot to have around. She was going to miss him like crazy.

12

MOTIVATED BY AN IMAGE of Bethany covered in fudge ripple, Nash made good on his boast. He tore up two-thirds of the carpet in the living room and carted it out to the bed of his truck. Bringing his crowbar back inside, he pried up all the tacking strips around the perimeter of the room and took those out to his truck, too.

He'd make a run to the dump tomorrow before the dinner. Mostly he tried not to think about the dinner. With the living room well on its way to being de-carpeted, he left Bethany to finish up while he tackled the master bedroom. It had a god-awful overhead fixture, too, which was actually fortunate because it let him see what he was doing.

Lamps. He'd forgotten about lamps for in here. But he had a bed coming, at least. Jack had let him use the computer in his office this afternoon to go online and see what Jackson furniture stores had to offer.

Jack had seemed to enjoy the search as much as Nash had. They'd found a beauty of a bed—a massive four-poster of dark wood that looked simple yet elegant. Because Nash needed everything—mattress, foundation, mattress pad, pillows, linens and a comforter, the store had given him a discount. The purchase still put a huge dent in his credit card, but he didn't care.

The bed was the first piece of furniture he'd bought since…well, for a long time. Lindsay had found sneaky yet devastating ways to make him aware that the pricey furniture filling their home in Sacramento had been thanks to her money. Or more accurately, her parents' money.

He'd told himself not to let that bug him, but it had. This bed represented a new direction in his life, and he'd decided in advance not to buy the cheapest thing he could find that would serve the purpose. Besides, he planned to make love to Bethany on it.

That wasn't the reason for choosing such a great bed, of course. She'd only be around a few more nights, so he'd be a fool to buy something that he thought she'd like. Even so, he *did* think she would like it, and he could hardly wait for them to try it out.

He'd arranged delivery for first thing in the morning and he'd meant to tell her that earlier. But the dinner discussion had made him forget. Having the bed come tomorrow would be good timing, though. After they'd made it successfully through that dinner, they could celebrate on his new king-size bed.

Pausing, he called out to her. "I ordered a bed today."

The ripping noise stopped in the living room. "You did? That's great."

"I scheduled delivery for tomorrow at ten. Will that work for you?"

"Sure." The ripping noise started up again. Then it stopped. "What's it like?"

He smiled, happy that she cared. Continuing to work,

he shouted over the racket because he was getting impatient for a serving of Bethany à la mode. "Oh, you know. Six feet square. Firm, but bouncy."

"Very funny." She kept working, too. "Just a foundation and mattress, then? No frame?"

"Who needs that? I can just throw it on the floor."

She appeared in the doorway. She was covered from head to foot in carpet dust. Her hair looked more brown than black, and smudges of dirt dappled her face, arms and legs.

She was the most beautiful mess he'd ever seen. He could make love to her right this minute, dirt and all, except he doubted that she'd let him near her. He was a disaster, too.

He'd taken off his shirt as promised and hung it on the back of a dining room chair to put on later. Consequently his torso was caked with dirt and sweat. He had carpet dust in his hair and it coated his jeans and boots as if he'd rolled in brown sugar. He figured the jeans and boots could be dusted off later, too.

"Please don't tell me you're going to put your foundation and mattress on the floor," she said.

"Why not? That works. Some sheets, a few pillows, a blanket, and I'm good to go."

"No, you're not! That's tacky. At least buy one of those metal frames on wheels. They're not expensive, and it'll keep your foundation from getting all ratty because it's on the floor instead of..." She narrowed her eyes at him. "You bought a bed frame, didn't you?"

He cracked up. "Of course I did. I'm not some teenager who's furnishing his first pad. I want a real bed, something substantial." He waggled his eyebrows. "Something that will stand up to whatever I throw at it."

"You're impossible."

"I know, and you're so much fun to tease."

"So what *did* you get?"

"You'll find out tomorrow."

"Nash!"

"Okay, okay. It's a four-poster, and the posts are dark wood and kind of plain, but they have some shape to them. They're thick, but graceful. You'll see."

"So you went into Jackson?"

"Nope. I used Jack's computer and found one on-line. He and I looked them over together. He approved of my choice, and considering that Jack's a connoisseur of fine beds, his stamp of approval means something."

"I'm eager to see it." Then she frowned. "But we have a problem."

"What problem? The delivery includes setup. I ordered sheets, and if you want to put those on, that would be great. It'll be all set up when we get back tomorrow night. We'll have room to spread out."

"But the floor in here won't be ready. I was thinking I'd rent a floor polisher tomorrow, but even if I made it back with the polisher before ten, I wouldn't have time to finish before the bed arrives."

"I see the problem. I was so eager to get it delivered that I forgot about the floor." He gazed at her as he considered the alternatives. "Okay, have them set it up in the living room for now. And don't worry about polishing the floor. That should be my job."

She shook her head. "I want to. I'm dying to see how it looks, so I don't think it's a hardship. But if they set it up, we'll just have to take it down to move it. Why not have them leave it boxed up? I'll finish the floor

tomorrow, and you and I can put the bed together tomorrow night."

"That makes sense, I guess." He shook his head
sadly. "Too bad we have that dinner. I figured after
it was over, we'd be ready to bounce around on that
bed and let off steam. Instead we'll have to construct
it first."

"Think of it as foreplay."

He grimaced. "I don't know how easy it'll be to as-
semble a bed when my johnson is sticking out like a
damned flagpole."

That made her laugh.

"Seriously! All through that interminable dinner
I'll be wishing I could be here having sex with you,
and when we finally make it through the door, the last
thing I'll want to do is put a bed together before I can
get some relief."

"Poor baby."

"Have them set it up in the living room."

"Is that an order?" She sounded amused.

"Yes. Yes, it is. We are going to come through that
front door, shuck our party clothes and christen my new
bed. End of story."

"All righty."

"Which brings me to the next item on the agenda.
Are you about finished in there?"

"Almost. Why?"

"Because I only need about five more minutes on this
room. Then I'll haul all the carpet and tacking strips
out to my truck and be ready to hit the showers. With
you. That can be our main course, and then we'll get
out the ice cream for dessert."

"You have this all mapped out, don't you?"

"Sweetheart, I've been dreaming about getting naked with you tonight ever since my eyes popped open at dawn. Get back to work so we can put this nasty chore behind us."

"You're giving orders again."

He winked at her. "That's because I'm getting agitated. But in a good way. Now move that sweet little fanny of yours."

Giving him a sloppy salute, she spun around and left. It was all he could do not to throw down his X-Acto knife and go after her. Dirt be damned. She had that kind of high-octane effect on him.

But if he didn't get all the carpet out, then she couldn't realize her dream of polishing the floor in here. She seemed really set on doing that, and so he kept working. He'd pulled up the last tacking strip when she reappeared in the doorway.

"I'm done," she announced.

"Me, too." He pushed himself to his feet. "I'll gather up everything and dump it in my truck. It might take two trips."

"Want me to help?"

He glanced down at her bare feet. "I can do it. Once I've hauled everything out to the truck, I'll strip down in the living room. Might as well keep the dirt contained as much as possible."

"Sounds like a plan." She helped load him up and held the front screen door for him.

He did have to make a second trip out to his truck, and when he returned from that, he was treated to the sight of Bethany taking off her clothes in the middle of the empty living room with the overhead light shining right down on her.

She glanced up as he came through the door, and there wasn't a shred of self-consciousness in her expression. Sometime in the past twenty-four hours, she'd become used to getting naked in front of him. He liked that.

"I just dropped everything on the floor," she said.

"So I see." His gaze drifted to the only clean places left—her nicely rounded breasts and the area protected by her shorts.

"I'll meet you in the bathroom," she said. "The water takes a while to warm up." She started to leave, which gave him a great view of her backside. There was something to be said for overhead lights.

"Wait." He leaned against the wall and pulled off one of his boots and his sock. "Let's go in together."

She turned back with a smile. "You won't get an argument from me. I like watching you take off your clothes."

"Likewise." He pulled off the other boot and sock.

"So I guess we're not shy with each other anymore." She followed his movements with her gaze as he unbuttoned his jeans and pulled down the zipper.

"No, guess not." Having her concentrate so intently on his crotch had a predictable result. When he shoved down his briefs and jeans, he released a very eager, very erect cock.

"I like looking at you, Nash. I've never let myself really look at a man before. I was afraid it would seem too...bold."

"I like bold women." He kicked away his jeans. "Shrinking violets bore me to tears."

"Lucky for me."

He walked toward her. "Lucky for me, too." Other

words ran through his mind, words that would point out
how perfect they seemed to be for each other. He didn't
say them. Instead he slid his gritty fingers through hers.
"Let's hit the showers, sweetheart."

"Gee, do you think we need it?"

"Nah." He walked through the dining room still holding her hand. "But it's the only way we'll have shower
sex."

"Don't forget that the pipes rattle something fierce.
I hope that doesn't spoil the mood."

"Not at all. That means you can yell as loud as you
want when I make you come, and nobody will hear
you."

"There's no one to hear me in the first place."

"Oh. Good point. Then I'll pretend the rattling pipes
are a drumroll signaling that your climax is about to
arrive."

She squeezed his hand. "Keep this up and I'll start
thinking the rattling pipes add to the value of the house."

"Nice try. I'm not paying extra for lousy plumbing."
Too bad she wouldn't be here when he fixed it.

Once they reached the bathroom, she insisted on
taking charge of the bathtub faucet because she knew
the bathtub's quirks. He watched her breasts quiver and
bob as she fiddled with the faucet to get the tempera-
ture right. His pride and joy remained as rigid as ever.
All it needed, apparently, was a little anticipation, and
it rose to the occasion.

Finally she straightened and drew back the shower
curtain. "After you."

"Oh, no. I want you in there first. I'm hoping you'll
do that sexy female thing."

"What sexy female thing?"

"You know, from the body-wash commercials. You turn your back to the spray, arch into it and slick your hair away from your face. But the commercials never show the good parts."

She rolled her eyes. "You're ridiculous."

"Will you do it? It gets me hot."

She glanced pointedly at his jutting penis. "You're already hot."

"Hotter, then. I promise I'll make it worth your while."

Shaking her head, she climbed into the tub.

When he climbed in after her, she was in the pose he'd requested, but she was shaking with laughter. "Bledsoe, you are such a dork. I don't know why I'm doing this."

"I'll show you." He began with her uplifted breasts, kissing and suckling each one. She wasn't laughing now, he noticed.

As the pipes clanked and groaned, he moved down her water-slicked body until he sank to his knees, spread his hands over her backside and angled his head until he was in a perfect position. Then he took command. In his estimation, her groans were actually louder than the noise coming from the pipes.

After two climaxes, she begged him to stop. "Or else I won't have any energy left for you," she murmured.

It was a convincing argument. He ached like he hadn't ached in years, and she had just the mouth to take care of that issue for him. They traded places, but he didn't bother to do the commercially inspired arch. With a guy, it lacked something.

As the water sluiced away all the dirt and dust that had collected on his body from the carpet project, she dropped to her knees in front of him and worked him over in a way that he would remember forever. She had such a talented mouth, such supple hands, and she cupped, squeezed, stroked and sucked.

Finally, nearly mad with the pounding in his groin, he clutched the back of her head and pleaded with her to take him all the way. He'd never asked for that in his life, but this was Bethany. She humbled him.

She also gave him what he asked for. He felt his cock touch the back of her throat. Her mouth had seemed so tender, so gentle, and yet she pulled an orgasm out of him that made him bellow with the sheer force of it. Panting, he fought to stay on his feet.

Somehow they managed to shut off the water and climb out of the tub without killing themselves. If he thought they'd do this ever again, he'd install grab bars. But it might be a singular event. Maybe that was for the best. Much more of this, and he'd beg her for more than an orgasm. He'd beg her to stay.

13

THEY NEVER MADE IT TO the ice-cream caper. Bethany suggested they save the experience for the next night and use the plastic covering that his mattress was shipped in to protect his new bed. He kept trying to convince her he was up for another round, but it didn't take a genius to see that he was exhausted.

He'd worked far harder on the carpet project than she had, and his day job was physically taxing, too. If he could have fallen asleep afterward, they might have indulged, but he had to drive back to the Last Chance. Everyone might know what was going on, but they didn't have to advertise the fact by having Nash drag in at dawn.

So once they'd both dried off, she pulled on a bathrobe and, in spite of his protests, went to get his clothes. By the time she'd taken his jeans out to the porch to give them a good shake and returned to the bedroom, he was sprawled on her bed, nearly asleep.

How she longed to tuck him in and leave him there. But she knew he wouldn't be happy about that in the morning. So she shook him awake and helped him get dressed. She worried that he was too groggy to drive.

"I can make coffee," she said.

He smiled sleepily. "I'll be fine. Nobody could fall asleep on that horrible road of yours. If you were selling to anyone but me, you'd have to get it graded. But I'll take care of it after..." His voice faltered. "After you leave."

"Okay." She didn't want to think about that any more than he did. Once she returned to her routine in Atlanta, she hoped her memory of him would fade. Right now she couldn't imagine that happening, but for her sanity, it had to.

"I'll pick you up at six." He lingered by her screen door.

"That's silly. I can drive over."

"Well, you *could,* but then what excuse would I have for coming back after dinner?"

"Oh." She liked knowing that his brain was functioning, which meant he'd be okay on the drive home. "But won't they all think it's strange that you came to get me instead of me just driving over there?"

"Not if we make a big deal about the condition of your road and the fact that you have a rental car."

"Nash, I drive the road all the time. I'll be driving it tomorrow when I go pick up the floor polisher."

He frowned at her. "You're not helping."

"Then why don't you simply say that picking me up is the gentlemanly thing to do?"

"Brilliant. Sarah will love that. She's big on manners. Thank you. Excellent suggestion. So I'll be here at six."

"What should I wear? Does everyone dress up?"

"Not in a big way. Nice jeans. Nice shirts. Sometimes the women wear something with a little sparkle to it."

"But I'm supposed to be a city girl, right?"

"Guess so. But I don't know what—"

"Never mind." She wasn't going to put the poor guy through any more discussion about her clothes selection. "I know what I'm going to wear. See you at six."

"Wish I didn't have to leave." He leaned down and gave her a soft kiss.

"Yeah, me, too." She watched him cross the porch and amble down the steps. When he reached his truck, he turned and waved as if he knew she'd still be standing there. Good instincts. "Drive carefully," she called out.

"I will." He climbed in his truck, started the engine and drove away, taking that nasty carpet with him. As his truck's red taillights disappeared around a curve, she battled the gnawing emptiness of missing him. With a sigh, she closed and locked the door. She'd have to get over that inconvenient feeling, but until she left for Atlanta, she might as well not even try.

After she turned off the overhead light in the living room, she expected the room to be plunged into darkness. Instead, moonlight spilled through the living room windows and lit up a section of the bare floor. She smiled to herself. Now she knew where the new bed was going.

As she slipped under the sheets of her own little bed, she gave thanks that plenty of hard work topped off with great shower sex allowed her to sink quickly into oblivion. Her sleep was filled with erotic dreams of Nash, and she woke up to a sunny day and the prospect of having a bigger bed delivered, one they could share for a little while tonight.

The two guys from Jackson who brought the bed were cheerful and friendly, although they complained about her road. They seemed puzzled by her request that they set up the bed in the empty living room, but they went along with it. After they left, Bethany admired the bed, standing boldly in the middle of the room, from all sides. She'd asked the guys to position it so the footboard faced the front door. She wanted Nash to get the full effect when he walked in tonight at six. But later on, when the lights were turned off, the bed would be bathed in moonlight.

The posts probably weren't actual walnut, but they were stained that color. About five feet high, they were nicely proportioned. The headboard was plain except for a groove that ran about three inches around the perimeter. The footboard had a similar groove.

Kicking off her sandals, she hopped up on the bed. It didn't move an inch. Then she bounced a little on the mattress. It gave, but the bed itself remained solidly planted on the floor. Nothing creaked. Yep, this was the perfect bed for sex.

Her thoughts strayed to Nash having sex on this bed with someone other than her, but she immediately banished the image. It was unproductive. "Happiness Is a Choice," she muttered to herself as she climbed off the bed, picked up one of the large plastic bags that held the linens and began opening packages.

A second bag contained two king-size pillows. If she'd been buying, she would have opted for several standard pillows instead of two humongous ones, but that was probably a woman thing. A guy would figure a king bed needed two king pillows.

She smiled when she discovered the sheets and pillowcases were white. Also probably a man thing. Or a Nash thing. She had no idea what his favorite color was, now that she thought about it. Or when his birthday was, or if he had a favorite TV show, or whether he liked to dance.

In some ways she knew him more intimately than she'd known any other man. But she had huge gaps in her knowledge of Nash Bledsoe. As she made up the bed, she thought about asking him some of those questions.

And yet, that might be a mistake. Why find out when his birthday was if she'd never celebrate it with him? They weren't destined to watch TV together, and his favorite color was of no consequence, either. Any yearning she had to learn more about him was evidence that she hadn't faced reality. They had no future.

For the next few nights, though, they had a really great bed. She'd told the delivery guys to leave the plastic they'd taken off the mattress. It lay folded in a corner in case ice cream came into play.

The snowy sheets and white down comforter gave her an idea. Shoshone didn't have a florist, but she'd noticed a red rosebush outside the Shoshone Diner. If they'd sell her a bloom or two, she could strew rose petals over the bed.

Several hours later, she had rose petals on the bed, and a waxed and polished master bedroom floor to show for her day's efforts. She hummed to herself as she stripped down for a shower. She'd laid a clingy black dress on her own little bed. It was part of the city-girl look she wanted to project at dinner tonight.

The clanking of the pipes almost drowned out the sound of her cell phone, but that ring was distinctive. She didn't take time to turn off the water as she dashed for the phone she'd left sitting on her pink-and-white dressing table.

When she answered, the expected cool voice came on the line. "Please hold for Miss Knightly." A thousand frantic thoughts ran through her head as she waited to hear Opal's Southern drawl. Whatever her mentor had on her mind was important or she wouldn't have called. They'd agreed that Bethany needed this week away from work so she could cut her ties to Jackson Hole.

"Bethany, honey. How are you doing, girlfriend?" Opal's deep voice, familiar to viewers all over the world, seemed to fill the little bedroom.

"I'm fine, Opal." Bethany took long, slow breaths. "What's up?"

"I need to inform you of something, but— What's that racket I hear in the background?"

"It's the plumbing."

"The *plumbing?* Heavenly days, it sounds like you're standing inside a cotton gin. Can you make it stop, or does it just do that all the time?"

"I can turn off the shower."

"Then do that, please. I can't think while that's going on."

"I'll be right back." Bethany laid down the phone, ran back to the bathroom and shut off the water. Her heart continued to pound and she was short on air as she hurried back and picked up the phone. "It's off."

"Praise the Lord. You need to get that fixed, honey."

"I know." Her stomach was in knots. Opal didn't ever call just to chat.

"Here's the problem." Opal's tone became more businesslike.

Bethany was afraid she'd pass out. "What problem?"

"My sources tell me that the folks at *Real News 24/7* think they might have a story on you."

"Oh, no." The hard-hitting show specialized in digging up unsavory details about celebrities. Bethany squeezed her eyes shut and prayed that Morgan hadn't slipped up, or worse yet, Nash. "How did they get it?"

"It seems that before he died, your dad raved a little about his daughter. Nobody believed the guy because he was often delirious, but a nurse talked to someone, who talked to someone else, and gradually a rumor that the author of *Living with Grace* had let her father die alone and in poverty made its way, like rumors often do, to *Real News* in New York."

"Dear God." Bethany sank to the edge of her bed and gulped for air.

"Don't panic, sweetie. It's not true, and you'll be vindicated. But I'd rather they didn't show up at the Triple G and find a dump. So is it one?"

Bethany felt light-headed. "Not exactly."

"What do you mean, *not exactly?* Is it just a little run-down, or does it look like it's got a date with the wrecking ball?"

Bethany gulped. "From the outside, it's kind of bad. We've been working on the inside of the house, but—"

"You know the importance of first impressions, honey. They'll film the outside and think they have their story. How fast can you get everything in shape?"

"I don't know. How long do I have?"

"Hard to say. I doubt they'll be out there tomorrow, but they might show up in a couple of days. Here's my advice. Hire as many people as you need to bring it up to snuff in the next twenty-four hours. If it's a money issue, then I can—"

"No, Opal. Thank you, but I can handle this." She had the money. The logistics were the problem, but Nash would help her figure it out. Just thinking of him calmed her frazzled nerves. "Thank God you heard about it."

"Honey, Opal Knightly sees all and knows all. And sometimes tells all." Her rich laughter spilled over Bethany like warm maple syrup. "Call me tomorrow, okay? I want to know what kind of progress you're making."

"I will."

"Good. Gotta run. Time for my massage. 'Bye, sugar."

"'Bye, Opal." She said it even though she knew Opal had hung up. *Thank God for Opal Knightly.* She owed that woman so much that she'd never be able to repay her kindness. Opal had invited her on the show when her first book had come out, and without that boost, Bethany's career might never have taken off.

But Opal hadn't stopped there. She'd continued to support Bethany's career and they'd become friends. Well, not the kind of friends who went shopping and hung out at coffee shops together, but the kind who respected each other's work and cared how each other's lives were going.

She'd confided in Opal as she'd tried to decide how to deal with her depressed father during the past eighteen months. She'd felt that if Opal was endorsing her career, she should know about the skeleton in Bethany's closet. Now that truthfulness had paid off.

Ironically, the new crisis had evolved from her father bragging about her to his caretakers. That knowledge wrapped her in a warm blanket of parental approval she'd never felt before, and tears slid down her cheeks. He had loved her, had been proud of her, and that filled an empty place in her soul. The invasion by *Real News* wasn't welcome. Still, evidence of her father's pride healed wounds she'd barely acknowledged, but had felt all the same.

Yet he'd left her with a big problem, and she had no idea how she'd pull off this miracle of giving the ranch a makeover in one day. Maybe Nash would have some ideas. *Nash!* She glanced at the time on her phone and tossed it on the bed. He would be here in twenty minutes, and she must not be late. That wouldn't start the evening off well.

Her shower was quick and her makeup application even quicker. She slipped on the dress, added a silver belt and silver hoop earrings and grabbed her black sling-back pumps just as she heard his truck pull in. Stepping into the pumps, she dashed into the living room as he walked through the screen door.

When he saw her, he stopped abruptly and stared in the way that all women longed for when they dressed up for a man. He didn't even glance at the bed. "Wow."

She'd hoped for a comment along those lines. "You said I should emphasize that I'm a city girl."

"You're emphasizing more than that, sweetheart." He walked slowly toward her. "I would kiss you, but I don't want to muss you up." His gaze raked over the flirty little dress. "And if I started kissing you, I'd want to muss you up." He made a soft growling sound.

She laughed, feeling suddenly lighter just because he was here. "How do you like the bed?"

"Oh." He turned toward it as if only now realizing it was there beside him. "Looks good. I hope you didn't rob some little old lady's garden to get the rose petals."

"I most certainly did not."

"So where're they from?"

"My secret."

His gaze flicked from the bed to her. "Damn. You and rose petals on a big ol' bed. I sure would love to—"

"Later."

"It'll seem like an eternity. But I guess we'd better go."

"Take a peek into the master bedroom first." She walked to the doorway and reached inside to flick on the overhead.

Nash whistled in approval. "You're not only sexy and honest, you polish up a floor real good. That looks terrific."

"I think so, too." She turned off the light. "I was planning to start on the living room tomorrow, but I'll have to postpone that job."

"Oh? Why?"

"I'll tell you on the way." She grabbed her purse from where she'd hung it on the back of the doorknob. "Want to do the honors of locking up?"

"Sure, why not?" He pulled his key, which was still attached to the Yellowstone National Park key ring, out of his pocket. "I've been carrying this around ever since you gave it to me. It makes the whole thing seem more real."

"I'm glad." Knowing how happy he'd be living here helped ease her sorrow about leaving at the end of the week. She walked out to the porch. "You washed your truck."

"Sure did. Vacuumed the inside, too. I can't show up for a date with a dirty truck, especially after I made such a big deal with Sarah that I was doing the gentlemanly thing by fetching you."

"So we're on our first official date?" She smiled at him as she navigated the uneven dirt of the yard in her pumps.

"I think this qualifies. You're a dinner guest at the Last Chance and I'm your escort. Let me get the door and help you in. That way I can ogle your legs."

She stuck her tongue out at him.

"Hey, I like that tongue routine. I read that as a potential French kiss coming up. Or maybe you're subtly suggesting that something even more exotic will happen with that tongue of yours before the night is over. This is going to be one hell of a first date."

She was laughing so hard she had trouble buckling her seat belt.

"I like it when you laugh," he said as he climbed into the driver's seat and closed the door. "You do this funny little hiccup thing that's sort of dorky but I like it." He started the engine and backed the truck around so it faced the road.

"I like it when you laugh, too," she said. "Sometimes you snort."

"I do *not*."

"Yeah, you do."

"Okay, maybe sometimes. But not a lot. Occasionally." Smiling, he turned to her. "Ready to lose a few fillings out of your teeth?"

"Go for it." Because the road was so bumpy, she decided to wait until they hit pavement before broaching her news. After he turned down the two-lane highway toward the Last Chance, she told him about Opal's call.

He listened intently and muttered a few swear words during the explanation.

"So there's my problem," she said. "Any ideas?"

"I'm thinking."

"Opal suggested I hire as many people as I need to, but I wouldn't know where to begin. I was hoping you could help me figure that out."

"I will, but since your cover is blown you might as well lay all this out at dinner and see if anyone has a suggestion."

She took a deep breath. "Guess you're right."

"You sound reluctant."

She glanced over at him. "I hadn't realized until now how much I've enjoyed being out of the spotlight for a few days. It's been fun being just…a woman spending time with a man."

Reaching over, he slid his fingers through hers. "I know what you mean." He gave her hand a squeeze.

Her throat tightened as she squeezed back. They might have a few stolen moments together after this, but it wouldn't be the same. That feeling of being cocooned from the world had ended, and she ached to have it back.

14

IN A WAY, NASH WAS RELIEVED that he wouldn't have to watch every word out of his mouth tonight. Sure as the world Sarah would keep everyone's wineglasses full, and he could easily forget and make some remark that revealed Bethany's secret. But that was a small thing, really, compared to the larger issue.

Their playtime was effectively over, and they both knew it. The world had intruded on their private relationship. If he'd worried about the dinner affecting things between them, that was nothing compared to the impending arrival of a news team with an attack-dog mentality.

He'd already decided to ask for the day off tomorrow so he could personally work at the Triple G. Under the circumstances, he thought Jack would give it to him. He hoped that the combined brainpower sitting at the dinner table tonight would figure out a way to transform the little ranch into a showplace, at least enough to fool a TV crew.

But that discussion had to wait until they were all gathered around the long dinner table in the Last

Chance's formal dining room. Located just off the large
dining room used for lunch with the hands, the more intimate one was lit by a Western-styled wood-and-metal
chandelier. The table had been set with polished silver,
gleaming crystal and cloth napkins. Nash smiled when
he saw the cloth napkins. Both Sarah and her cook,
Mary Lou, insisted on them.

Surprisingly, it was an adults-only gathering tonight.
Taking her usual seat at the end of the table with Pete on
her right, Sarah announced that Emmett and Emily had
organized a cookout for the youth-program boys and
had roped Emily's husband, Clay, into helping. Luke
Griffin had volunteered to babysit the grandkids upstairs.

Nash and Bethany sat across the table from his mother
and stepfather. So far Lucy had been friendly but cau-
tious toward Bethany. Ronald had followed her lead.

All three of the Chance boys were there with their
wives, which was always a treat for Nash. He might not
have lucked out in the matrimony department, but his
friends had. His buddy Jack had shown great taste when
he'd hooked up with Josie. Gabe was obviously crazy
about his wife, Morgan, and Nick, the middle son, had
found the perfect match in Dominique.

Just last summer the family had expanded to include Jack's half brothers on his mother's side. Diana,
the woman who'd abandoned Jack as a toddler and cut
off all contact, had remarried and produced twin boys,
Wyatt and Rafe. Nash had come in on the tail end of the
drama that had ensued when Jack discovered he had
two more brothers.

But everyone had adjusted, and even the wayward
Diana, now divorced, was allowed to pay periodic vis-

its to the Last Chance. She wasn't here tonight, though, and Nash was grateful for that. Chaos seemed to follow that woman, and they didn't need additional problems.

Wyatt, who owned an adventure trekking company, was leading a group through Yellowstone and his wife, Olivia, had tagged along. Rafe and his fiancée, Meg, were at the dinner table, though. Nash got a kick out of how Rafe, a city slicker from San Francisco, had gone country. Looking at him now, no one would suspect he hadn't been born and bred in Jackson Hole.

Seeing all the happily-ever-afters gathered around the table made Nash wish for his own…with Bethany. It was a futile wish, considering her high-profile career, although her earning power didn't bother him anymore. She wasn't Lindsay and would never lord finances over him. But that didn't matter. Her life was elsewhere.

Sarah raised her wineglass. "A toast to our former neighbor, Bethany Grace, and to our new neighbor, Nash Bledsoe."

"Hear, hear!" Jack lifted his glass in Nash's and Bethany's direction.

Everyone else followed suit, including his mother and stepfather. Nash smiled at them in appreciation for their acceptance of the situation. His mother might wish that he had a good woman to love as well as a ranch of his own, but that would have to wait.

"Thank you all for inviting me tonight," Bethany said. "As it turns out, I desperately need your advice."

Nash pressed his knee against hers under the table to subtly give her moral support.

She described the situation, not sugarcoating any of it, but not blaming her father, either. In fact, the bitter-ness she'd displayed toward him when Nash had first met her seemed to have disappeared. Nash was glad about that.

"I need a lot of work done and I only have one day to do it," Bethany said. "I'm happy to pay the going rate, but I don't know who will be available on such short notice."

"That's easy." Jack's dark eyes glittered in a way that Nash recognized. His buddy loved a challenge. "We'll do it."

"You?" Bethany stared at him. "But you all have a ranch to run, and a million things to do, and—"

"And it can wait one day," Sarah said. "Jack, if you hadn't said it, I would have."

"And if he hadn't, I would have," Gabe added.

Nick laughed. "I doubt I would have gotten a word in edgewise, but I'm all for it. We can take most of the hands over there, too."

Nash had never been so proud of his friends in his entire life. He'd hoped they'd have suggestions. He'd never expected this, but it fit with the kind of people they were.

"I'd like to offer those eight boys," Pete said. "They're not skilled, but they're eager, and this would teach them the value of being a good neighbor and helping someone out in a time of need. They can fetch and carry while everyone else works. I'll supervise them."

"I'll help, too," Ronald said. "I'm still a fair hand with a hammer."

Nash's mother looked across the table at him. "I can paint like nobody's business. And I know what color you want on those outbuildings, too, Nash Bledsoe. Dark red."

He gave his mother a big grin. "Thanks, Mom. But

I'll take whatever color's available. This isn't the time for me to be picky."

"It is, too. It's going to be your ranch. You might as well get it fixed the way you want it."

"So, Bethany." Sarah directed a question at her. "Will this work for you?"

Nash glanced over at her. Tears brimmed in her eyes, and when she nodded rapidly, a couple spilled onto her cheeks.

He put his arm around her and gave her a quick hug. He didn't give a damn who took note of that, either.

She sniffed and wiped away her tears. "I don't know what to say." Her voice was choked. "I...I'm over-whelmed."

Josie's voice was gentle. "Say yes. I've learned that when the Chance family takes you under their wing, you'd best settle in and prepare to be gifted by their gen-erosity. They can't help themselves. It's in the genes."

"That's right." Dominique nodded in agreement.

"In other words," Morgan said, "relax and enjoy it."

"Then...thank you all. Thank you from the bottom of my heart."

Sarah smiled at her. "It's our pleasure, Bethany." Then she turned back to the rest of the group. "Eat up, everybody. After the meal, we should all drive over to the Triple G and assess the situation."

"What a great idea!" Nash's mother clasped her hands together in obvious joy. "I'll get to see the house my boy will be living in."

Nash hoped he was the only one who'd heard Beth-any suck in a breath. He wondered if she was think-ing the same things he was. First of all, the charred remains of the recliner still sat in the front yard. Nash had never told anyone at the Last Chance about the flaming recliner.

The chair stood in mute testimony to the depth of Bethany's anger at her father. Nash thought maybe her feelings had mellowed, which might make her even more embarrassed to let the Chance family see that chair. But he doubted that was the only reason she didn't want everyone trooping over to the Triple G tonight.

They couldn't deny this group a peek into the house after this outpouring of goodwill. But anyone walking through the front door would find a very large bed covered in rose petals. Bethany was leaving at the end of the week, but Nash wasn't, and he'd never live this down. Jack would make sure of it.

ONCE BETHANY WAS BACK in the truck with Nash, she started plotting their strategy as they led the parade of vehicles to the Triple G. "Park right next to the front porch and block the steps if you can. Then distract everybody while I run in and scoop up those blasted rose petals."

"I don't think you'll have time to get them all. Besides, the bed will still be there, all made up and ready to go. We're not fooling anybody, Bethany."

She sighed and flopped back against the seat. "I know that, but we don't have to rub their noses in the fact that we're having sex."

"You can't do anything about the bed, so I say let's brave it out. In fact, leave the rose petals. Then at least my mother will have to acknowledge there's romance involved. Without the rose petals, it's just sex. With them, it's romantic sex."

"It's still extremely embarrassing. I love how everyone's willing to help, but I wish they weren't coming over *tonight*. I shouldn't have made the bed. If I'd left the sheets in the package, and—"

"Nope, it's better this way. My mother's a sucker for the romantic touch. So is everybody at the ranch, come to think of it."

"So you're planning to let *everyone* come in the house?" Bethany started to sweat. "I thought only your mother wanted to see it."

"She's the one who spoke up, but Morgan will want to get a look at the floor, and next thing you know, they'll all parade in there. Might as well be prepared for that."

She swallowed and pressed her hand against her tummy to quell the butterflies. "I suppose I should get used to this kind of thing. Once I'm a regular on Opal's show, people will be more curious than ever about my personal life."

"It's the price of fame, so they say." Nash's comment sounded sympathetic.

"And I have no business complaining about it. Plenty of people would love to have the success I've had. Not many people feel the touch of Opal's wand. I'm extremely lucky."

He chuckled and reached over to squeeze her knee. "Yeah, but you're allowed to be uncomfortable having everyone stare at the bed and the rose petals. And you can be cranky once in a while, too, without the world coming to an end. I'll never forget the picture of you standing in front of that burning recliner, your arms folded, pleased as hell with the destruction you'd created."

"Good Lord! The recliner is still there!"

"Ah, roll with it. They're fully aware your dad was no model parent. They'll understand."

"But that's just it. Now that I know he spent his last days raving about how great I am, I don't feel the same way about him. I'm not angry anymore."

"That's wonderful, Bethany." He gave her a quick smile. "Really terrific."

"Yes, but everyone will see that recliner, and they'll think—"

"That you're human. That sometimes you lose your temper, just like the rest of us."

"I hope so." She sighed. "That's why I feel at ease with you, Nash. You've seen the burning recliner, so I don't have to pretend that I'm happy every moment of the day. Believe me, when the world knows your motto is Happiness Is a Choice, you feel an obligation to be constantly happy because supposedly you found the answer."

"But you didn't?"

"I thought I did, but…maybe it's not so easy."

He blew out a breath. "Thank you. You have no idea how glad I am to hear you say that. Because I don't find it so damned easy. It *sounds* simple to say Happiness Is a Choice. But then life happens, and it's…not easy."

"I know. I need to write another book and talk about all I've learned since the last book."

"That's one I'd like to read."

She wondered if he would. Maybe she'd send him one. And maybe she wouldn't. As she'd told herself before, a clean break would be best.

"Well, here we are, sweetheart."

"Sorry about the rose petals, Nash. I bet you'll hear about them for months, if not longer."

"At first I worried about that. Jack loves to tease his friends. But you know what? I have a beautiful woman who thinks enough of me to toss rose petals on my bed. That's not embarrassing. In fact, it makes me look like a real stud."

As usual, he made her laugh. "Okay, then. The rose petals stay. Also, can you leave your headlights on and point them at the recliner? I'm going to make a speech about it."

"You are?" He seemed surprised.

"You've inspired me to be honest with everyone instead of being so worried about my image."

"Good for you." He steered the truck so the headlights focused on the recliner. "Go get 'em, tiger."

Buoyed by his support, she climbed down from the truck and stood by the blackened hulk. As everyone piled out of their vehicles and gazed at her with obvious curiosity, she raised her voice. "You're probably wondering what this is. Besides Nash, Morgan's the only one who's seen it, but she was too polite to comment."

"It seemed like a personal situation," Morgan said. "I thought you'd have hauled it away by now."

"It is a personal situation. When I first got here, I was so angry at my father for drinking himself to death that I dragged his old recliner, which stunk of booze, out of the living room and into the yard. Then I doused it with gasoline and torched it."

"Damn, woman," Jack said. "Remind me not to tick you off."

That brought a laugh from everyone, which eased the tension.

"I'm not proud of losing my temper like that, but it shows I'm not perfect. Neither was my dad, but I love him anyway. And besides, the smoke brought Nash over here, and meeting him was…very special. So now I look at this burned chair as evidence that we all have a dark side. It's also the reason I met Nash Bledsoe, and now, on top of that, I've met all of you. My dark side produced lots of benefits."

"That's touching," Lucy said. "I'm glad you told us."

"I agree it's a touching story," Jack said. "But that thing is butt-ugly. Did you have some plan for keeping it as a permanent souvenir? Have it bronzed, maybe?"

Bethany grinned at Jack. "It's a thought, but no. I don't think bronzing would improve the look. I'm growing fond of it, but I don't think it belongs in the front yard anymore."

"That's a relief. I was afraid we'd have to figure out how to dress it up pretty for the cameras. Okay, first thing tomorrow, when we have on our work clothes, we're hauling it…somewhere."

Nash turned off the headlights and stepped down from his truck. "I volunteer for that job." He walked over to Bethany and lowered his voice. "Nice speech."

"Thanks." She might have said more, but Lucy came toward her.

"Now that the chair business is settled, Bethany, can I see the house?"

"Sure thing." *One down, one to go.* Bethany maintained her bravado until the moment when Lucy walked through the front door. When Nash's mother lifted her eyebrows, Bethany wanted to run and hide in the back of the house until everyone had left.

But that would be cowardly, so she stood her ground. As did Nash, and she appreciated that.

Lucy's gaze, her blue eyes so like Nash's, took in

the bed from head to foot. It paused on the scattering of rose petals, and the corners of her mouth lifted. Not a lot, but a little.

Then she looked straight at Bethany. "All I ask is that you not break my boy's heart."

"I would never want to do that, Mrs. Hutchinson." She'd figured out that Lucy had taken Ronald's last name and was no longer using "Bledsoe."

"Considering your close relationship to my son, you ought to call me Lucy."

"Thank you…Lucy." She'd never been a mother, and her own mom had not been protective, but Lucy was. Bethany was a little in awe of Lucy and certainly didn't want to become her enemy. She had no desire to break Nash's heart, just as she knew he had no desire to break hers. But there would be pain when they parted. Nobody could keep that from happening.

"Are you going to show me the rest of the house?"

"Absolutely." With a glance at Nash, who covertly gave her a thumbs-up, she escorted Lucy on a minitour. Behind her, she heard Nash welcoming the rest of the Chance family into the house.

If she hadn't been so tense, she would have laughed. They'd supposedly come to evaluate how much work needed to be done to the exterior, but everyone seemed far more interested in this little house. As Nash bragged about the work she'd done on the floor in the master bedroom, she had the oddest feeling that the two of them were showing off their shared dwelling to visitors. For a few days, it had been theirs.

But soon it would belong to him and she'd no longer have the right to walk through these rooms. Thinking of that, she looked at everything with more fondness than

she'd ever done before. After all, for more than half her
life, it had been home.

At long last, the crowd of people headed outside.
Bethany had never bothered to hook up the spotlights
she'd bought to help Nash work after dark. They had
become superfluous. But the Chance crew had come
armed with powerful flashlights and everyone huddled
as they discussed what needed to be done.

Finally Jack broke away from the group and came
toward her. "We should start at first light."

"That's fine. I'm sure I'll be up."

He hesitated. "It'll be quite an onslaught. I hope
you're ready for that. This place has been deserted for
some time."

"Jack, you and your family, and Nash's family, are
lifesavers. Go for it."

Lucy approached. "I've been thinking that if those
newspeople want to go inside the house, you should
move that bed. Otherwise it's liable to end up on TV."

Bethany managed to keep a straight face. "I agree.
It's going in the master bedroom."

"But that leaves you with an empty living room."

"Can't be helped. The old furniture was hideous.
Better nothing than what was there."

"Since Ronald and I combined households, we have
several pieces we don't need. Nash may not want to keep
them forever, but we'll bring them over, so you can fill
up the space and make it look homey."

"Thanks, Lucy." Bethany smiled at her. "That would
be wonderful. Give me until nine in the morning, and
I'll have the living room floor polished for you."

"I can tell you're a hard worker. I've always admired
that." She glanced at Nash, who was in conversation

with Jack. Then she edged closer and lowered her voice. "Is there any way you could commute back and forth?"

"No, there isn't."

"I only ask because my daughter, Katrina, works in New York State, and she travels with the thoroughbred racing circuit. Her fiancé, Ronald's son, is constantly on the go with his photography. I don't know when and if Hutch and Katrina will settle in one place, but they're making a go of it. So I wondered if you and Nash…"

"His life is here and mine is there. We live far apart and we're both tied to our locations. I don't see how we could manage a relationship."

The soft light of hope died in Lucy's eyes. "I had to ask."

"Of course you did." Impulsively, Bethany gave her a hug. "I can see how much you love him."

"And so do you."

The direct statement caught her off guard. "I…probably could, but I haven't allowed myself to."

"Bull."

Bethany's eyes widened. "Excuse me?"

"You love him. I've lived long enough to recognize the signs. You watch him when you think he doesn't know it. Your expression goes all soft when he looks at you. You put rose petals on his bed. And he's in the same fix. That's why I'm worried. You say you don't intend to break his heart, but I don't see how you can avoid it."

Despair swamped her. "I have to avoid it. The last thing I want to do is hurt him."

"Then stay."

"Oh, Lucy, you don't know what you're asking. Have you ever watched Opal's show?"

"Never miss it. Have a TV in the back of the ice-cream parlor. She's a wonderful person."

"Opal's supported me from the day I released my first book. She's arranged for me to have a permanent segment on her show. She's one of the most powerful women in America, and she's thrown that influence behind me and my career. Tell me, would you turn your back on that?"

Lucy frowned in concentration. "I don't know. I've never had one of the most powerful women in America endorse my ice cream and offer me a TV gig. I'll have to think about that and get back to you."

"Fair enough."

"Which reminds me. Did that boy of mine bring you the fudge ripple I sent?"

"He did."

"What did you think?"

"Lucy, I'll tell you the honest truth. We didn't get around to opening it."

She smiled. "When you do, let me know your opinion. It's my favorite, so I thought I was safe in sending it as a gift. But you may be one of those people who can't abide chocolate."

"I'm not one of those people."

"Good. Then I think we can be friends."

"I think we can." Bethany didn't know how that could work out in the long run, but she was more than happy to be friends with Lucy until the inevitable happened and she and Nash broke each other's hearts. At that point, Lucy would never forgive her. Bethany wouldn't blame her a bit.

15

NASH WAS DETERMINED to wait everybody out so he could be alone with Bethany. But as sometimes happened in gatherings of this sort, no one seemed willing to be the first to leave. Finally Nash went over to Jack. "I don't mean to seem ungrateful and all, but could you get this herd moving?"

Jack adjusted the tilt of his black Stetson. "Have plans, do you?"

"Some."

"I would hope so. That's one hell of a bed. And it has rose petals on it."

"Yeah, I noticed. Listen, thanks for helping me order it. And, Jack, I appreciate you and your brothers stepping up tonight."

"Ah, you know the Chance boys. We live for this kind of drama. It's us against the smarmy greenhorns who want to make the good people of Jackson Hole look bad. We can't have that around here."

"I know Bethany was touched."

Jack glanced in Bethany's direction. "She's a nice

lady. I'd have thought, with all that Bledsoe charm, you could've convinced her to stick around."

"Even if I could, I wouldn't. She has a golden opportunity to become a really big television personality. What kind of guy would mess with that?"

Jack nodded. "Good point. Which means you need to maximize what little time you have with the charming Miss Grace."

"Exactly. That said, I'm staying the night."

"With a woman like Bethany and a bed like that one, I can't imagine why you wouldn't. We'll be out of your way shortly."

"Thanks, Jack." He watched in admiration as his buddy maneuvered the group in his own teasing style. He made a joke here, a provocative suggestion there, and within ten minutes, everyone had waved goodbye, piled into their vehicles and started down the bumpy road to their respective homes and beds.

Bethany walked over to him. "You put Jack up to that, didn't you?"

"I couldn't very well ask them all to leave after what they're proposing to do tomorrow. But he could." Nash captured her hand in his and started toward the house. "Let's go examine that bed."

"You have good friends, Nash."

"The best."

"I know they're doing this more for you than for me, but their willingness to help my cause is amazing. My dad wasn't the least bit neighborly, and they don't really know me at all."

"They know you." He walked with her up the creaky porch steps. By tomorrow night, after the Chance boys had finished with this place, the steps wouldn't creak.

"They know that you chose to sell the ranch to me instead of some stranger who might tear it down and build God-knows-what. Your concern for the history and the future of the Triple G is all the recommendation they need to classify you as good people."

"Before I got here, I was sure I'd be able to sell it without a second thought."

He opened the screen door and ushered her inside. "Then I guess you learned something about yourself this week." Closing the door, he twisted the lock. She didn't seem to notice that he'd locked them in.

"I learned a *lot* about myself this week." She nestled against him. "I can let that chair go, but I'll never forget it."

"I'm not taking it to the dump." He tilted his hat back and pulled her close.

"You're not? But you said you'd handle the job."

"And I will. I haven't figured out exactly what I want to do with it, so until I do, I'll haul it out to a back pasture and leave it for now."

"You're crazy, Nash Bledsoe."

"Yeah." *Crazy about you.* But he wouldn't say that and mess up a good thing. "Listen, I know we talked about playing around with ice cream tonight."

"I kept the shipping plastic if you still want to."

He looked into her beautiful gray eyes. God, he was going to miss her. "I think, considering how the bed looks so nice all fixed up with rose petals and clean sheets, that we should just…"

She reached up and took off his hat. "I agree. But indulge me with one thing, cowboy."

"What's that?"

"I'll show you." Easing out of his arms, she turned

and sent his hat sailing toward the farthest bedpost. I
dropped neatly down as if she'd been practicing the
move for hours.

"Good aim!"

"Lucky throw. But I've always wanted to do that."

He smiled, more charmed by her than she'd ever
know. "Glad I could accommodate you. Anything else
I can do to make your wishes come true?"

"Oh, I think there are plenty of things. But first, let
me set the stage." She walked over to the wall switch
and turned off the overhead.

"Wait." He peered into the darkness where she was
standing. "I can't see you."

"Look at the bed."

He shifted his attention, and sure enough, moonlight showcased the white bed as if someone were up
in a booth directing the scene. "How did you know that
would happen?"

"I noticed where the moonlight fell last night and
made sure that's where the guys set up the bed."

"Nicely done. But I still can't see you." His eyes
were adjusting slowly, but she must have moved back
into the shadows. He heard rustling noises that indicated she was up to something. "I'd rather look at you
than an empty bed."

"I thought you might." A gloriously naked Bethany
stepped out of the shadows and sashayed over to the
bed. Nudging back the covers, she slipped under the
white sheets as rose petals fluttered around her. The
edge of the sheet almost covered her breasts, but not
quite. A rose petal drifted into her cleavage and quivered with each breath she took.

Nash was transfixed.

"Care to join me, cowboy?"

"Yes." But when he'd dressed for dinner, he'd decided against tucking condoms in his jeans pocket. He didn't want to take a chance that he might shove his hands in his pockets during the evening and accidentally dislodge one. "But first I have to get—"

"This?" She held up a small foil package.

"Where did that come from?"

"I hid one under the pillow so it would be handy."

He started laughing as he pulled off his boots and shucked his clothes. "And you were worried about rose petals. What if my mother had decided to check to see if I bought goose down or polyester?"

"She'd do that?"

"Maybe. She loves goose-down pillows and might have wondered if I'd splurged on some."

"Then I guess your mother would have discovered that we practice safe sex."

"And she'd be proud." He tossed the last of his clothes to the floor and walked into the patch of moonlight that contained all he wanted in the world. "But I'm going to stop talking about her now, if it's all right with you." He slid into bed beside her.

"What do you want to talk about?"

"I don't want to talk at all." He ran his hand over her satiny skin.

"Do you want me to talk?"

"No." He cupped her breast as his lips hovered over hers. "I want you to moan."

And so she did. Often and deeply. He made love to her with an intensity far greater than it had been before, because now he could see the end. Tomorrow the Chance brigade would arrive on their doorstep, and after that, no doubt a news team would show up ready to rake some muck. He and Bethany might have more intimate moments like this, but he wouldn't bet on it.

He kissed every square inch of her he could reach, and then he had her turn over so he could cover that territory, too. He coaxed her to come with his fingers and with his mouth. Finally, when he couldn't stand the ache in his groin any longer, he eased her onto her back. Putting on a condom, he sank into her hot, wet center.

"At last!" She clutched his hips and pulled him in tighter. "This is what I want, Nash. This!"

Braced on his forearms and cradling her head in his hands, he looked into her moonlit eyes. "It's what I want, too," he murmured as he began to move. Being close, holding her, loving her, was all he could ever want.

Because he couldn't tell her so, he said nothing more, but he held her gaze and talked to her with his body. The easy strokes were a promise never to forget what they'd shared. The deeper, more powerful thrusts spoke of his passion. And at last he pounded into her until they both came in a fiery explosion of need. His ultimate surrender as he convulsed within her…was a declaration of love.

But at the end, he was afraid she'd see too much in his expression. He pressed his face into the hollow of her shoulder as the shudders wracked his body. He needed her so much. So very much.

She held him as if she'd never let him go. "I don't want you to leave." Her voice was hoarse. "I know it's late, but I can't bear the thought of you getting out of this bed."

He lifted his head and pillowed his cheek on her

breast. "I'm not leaving." He dragged in air. "I told Jack I was staying."

"Oh, good." She hugged him tighter. "So we have all night."

"Mmm-hmm." He lifted his head and looked into her eyes again. "Think you can handle that?"

"Slide your hand under the pillow and you'll see that I can."

He followed her directions and touched another foil packet, and another, and another. "Good God, woman, how many did you stash under here?"

"A few."

"You must think I'm some kind of stallion." And that was great for the ego.

"Aren't you?"

"Yeah, honey cakes." Smiling, he leaned down and kissed her. "Yeah, I am."

THEY TESTED THAT KING bed thoroughly throughout the night. They slept a little and made love a lot. Bethany worried that she might be tired the next morning, but either the bed was magic or Nash was, because she woke up refreshed and excited to start the day. So did he, and they made the discovery they were both morning people.

Working together, they stripped the bed and dismantled it. When they both admitted the new sheets had felt a little stiff, Bethany threw them in the washing machine while they reassembled the bed in the master bedroom. They worked quickly because the sun was coming up and that meant the Last Chance crew could arrive any minute. Bethany cooked breakfast while Nash made the recliner disappear.

She didn't ask him where he'd taken it and he didn't volunteer the information. His sentimentality about that chair now rivaled hers, and it made her heart ache. No two ways about it, he was going to be devastated when she left.

But she didn't have much time to fret about that, because right after they'd finished eating their scrambled eggs and had gulped down some coffee, the renovation crew arrived. The trucks came packed with people and supplies. Under Jack's direction, lengths of two-by-fours were unloaded from the backs of pickups and sawhorses were quickly set up by the barn.

In no time the air was filled with the sounds of nail guns and power saws. Jack had obviously put himself in charge of the operation and he seemed to be in his element directing the troops. Then Pete pulled in with a vanload of kids and set them to work making sure everyone had what they needed, whether that was a drink of water or a screwdriver. He assigned each boy to a cowhand until he ran out of boys and had to double up on a few.

"We're the slaves," a tattooed kid said to Bethany as he sprinted past. "I'm Mr. Bledsoe's slave." But he was grinning with pride as he said that. Being assigned to Nash had apparently been a hit with him.

Although Bethany would have loved to stay outside and work alongside Nash and the rest of the crew, she remembered that she'd promised to have the living room floor ready by nine. She'd barely finished when Lucy knocked on the screen door. "We're here!"

Bethany went out to the porch, where she discovered Ronald Hutchinson letting down the tailgate of a pickup loaded with furniture. "Goodness! Did you leave anything for yourselves?"

"Of course we did," Lucy said. "Once I moved in with Ronald, his house looked like something out of that television show about hoarders. It'll be nice to walk around without bumping into things."

"I'm sure Nash will be thrilled. Thank you."

Lucy glanced down toward the barn. "It's already looking good down there. I brought a whole bunch of dark red paint, too, just the shade he likes. It's called Barn Red."

Bethany followed the direction of her gaze to where Nash labored with the rest of the men. Sarah and the wives had shown up, too.

"You'd think they were at a party the way they're all laughing and having a good time," Lucy said.

"I know." Bethany wasn't sure how to handle her deep yearning to be a part of the festivities. Oh, sure, she could go down there and work with them today, but that would be it. No point in trying to fit in when she was on the brink of leaving.

By noon, an amazing amount of progress had been made on all fronts. The inside of the house looked quite lovely now that the living room had some decent furniture in it. The barn was getting a coat of Barn Red, and Emmett Sterling, the Last Chance's foreman, had arrived with rosebushes to plant in the front yard.

Then Mary Lou showed up with food, and everyone took a break to share the meal and admire the work that had been accomplished so far. Nash brought his plate over and sat on the porch steps so he could eat with Bethany, Lucy and Ronald.

"It might look like a three-ring circus," he said, "but

I think we'll actually get the place looking decent before the sun goes down."

"Have you seen the furniture your mom and Ronald brought over?" Bethany asked.

"No." He put down his plate and hopped onto the porch to go look. "I forgot all about that." He opened the screen door and whistled in approval. "Outstanding." He turned to smile at them. "You're awesome. I'll give it back once I have a chance to buy a few things, but this is great."

"Don't give it back to us," Lucy said. "It's yours until you pass it on to someone else. We're done with it."

"Wow, thanks. I—" He stopped talking and looked down the road. "Here comes somebody. And unless I'm seeing things, they're driving a black limo. Must be an idiot to try and bring a limo down that road."

Bethany's heart raced. "Are you sure it's a limo?"

"Yep. They're creeping along, though. It'll take a while before they pull in."

Bethany stood and took a deep breath. "Well, everyone, get ready. This party just got a little more interesting."

Nash glanced at her, his expression puzzled. "You sound as if you know who's in that car."

"I do." She wondered if Nash would realize that this truly was the end of their special time together. "You're all about to meet Opal Knightly."

16

NASH GLANCED DOWN AT HIS CLOTHES. He was covered with construction dust, but he couldn't do much about that. Everyone else was in the same condition. He took off his hat, ran his fingers through his sweaty hair and put the hat back on. It was the best he could do on short notice.

Although he didn't watch Opal's show, he had no trouble recognizing the woman who stepped out of the limo. He'd seen her face on a bunch of magazine covers over the years. A well-endowed blonde with a famous hourglass figure, she was his idea of the perfect Southern belle. Judging from her smooth skin, she could be any age from twenty-five to fifty, but she'd been on TV for quite a while, so she had to be at least mid-forties.

Her uniformed limo driver helped her out of the long black car, which was covered with a fine film of dust. Opal, however, had not a hair out of place. She wore a pink flowered dress, enough gold jewelry to open a small boutique and pink stilettos. Oversize sunglasses covered her famous green eyes.

Bethany hurried over to greet her. "I can't believe

you're here! Did you try to call? I might've missed the ring. I've been—"

"I didn't call, honey. I knew you'd tell me not to come." She took off her sunglasses and reached out to hug Bethany.

"Oh, you shouldn't. I'm a mess!"

"Of course you are." Opal embraced her protégée despite her protests. "You've been working hard."

Nash's opinion of the talk show host shot up considerably. She was treating Bethany as a friend, not some puppet she was manipulating for her own benefit. No wonder Bethany was so loyal to her.

Bethany accepted the hug and seemed moved by the gesture. "I wish you'd called, though."

"You know me, girlfriend." She winked. "I love me some drama." She glanced around at the crowd that had gathered. "But can you afford all these people, honey? Even at minimum wage, you're looking at a big bill."

"They're doing it for free."

Opal's carefully plucked eyebrows rose. "They *are*? How come?"

"Because that's the kind of people they are." She turned toward Sarah. "First of all, you need to meet Sarah Chance."

Sarah stepped forward and extended her hand. "Ms. Knightly, it's a pleasure. My sons and I own the Last Chance Ranch next door. We rounded up our family members and ranch hands to come over here today and see what we could accomplish."

"Quite a bit, looks like." Opal shook her hand. "I'm pleased to meet you, Sarah Chance. And let's not be formal. Call me Opal."

"We're honored to have you visit us, Opal."

"I was worried about my girl, here, but obviously I didn't need to be. I see that neighbors help neighbors out West the same as we do down South. You must think a lot of Bethany."

"We do." Sarah looked over at Nash. "Especially after she decided to sell her ranch to one of our own."

"Oh? And which one is that, Bethany?"

Bethany turned to Nash, her eyes bright. "I'm selling it to Nash Bledsoe. He's from this area and he's agreed to buy the Triple G."

Nash saw the warmth in her gaze and heard it in her voice, but maybe he was the only one tuned in to that. He hoped so. He stepped forward and touched the brim of his hat. "Pleased to meet you, ma'am."

Opal's gaze was assessing, but she flashed her famous smile. "And I'm delighted to meet you. This should take the wind out of *Real News*'s sails, having a local boy snap up what will soon be a picture postcard of a ranch. I like it."

"And this is Nash's mother, Lucy Hutchinson," Bethany said.

Nash blessed her for that. No doubt his mother was dying to meet her first-ever celebrity.

Lucy darted toward Opal and stuck out her hand. "Lucy Hutchinson. I've watched your show for years. And even though I wish Bethany and Nash could—"

"Hey, you know what?" Nash took his mother gently by the shoulder and drew her away from Opal and the train wreck she was headed for. "We've all been making our guest stand in the hot sun without offering her a bit of shade and something cool to drink."

Opal's knowing glance rested for a moment on Nash, and then her polished smile appeared again. "That sounds wonderful." She looked over at her chauffeur. "I'm sure Emile would appreciate that, too."

"Then please come inside with me," Bethany said.

Nash kept a firm grip on his mother as Bethany ushered Opal and her chauffeur toward the porch steps. Before Bethany went inside, she threw him a grateful glance. He gave her what he hoped was an encouraging smile.

"I shouldn't have said that, should I?" His mother turned to face him. "I'll admit it. I was starstruck. And I wanted her to know that I understood that she was offering Bethany a wonderful opportunity, and so if that meant that you and Bethany couldn't be together, well, that was life. But I shouldn't have gone into it, at least not right now."

"You shouldn't go into it ever, Mom." But he couldn't be angry with her. She'd met one of her idols, and that could cause anyone to lose their mind temporarily and say stupid things. "Opal doesn't need to know anything about what's been between Bethany and me."

His mother looked up at him. "You sound as if it's over already. But Bethany's still here."

"Yes, but so is Opal. She came to protect Bethany from the *Real News* people, which is something we don't have the power to do. We can fix up the place so they can't get any shots of a run-down ranch, but they could still hound Bethany about her father. They won't do that with Opal around. I'm glad she came."

"Even if it means you can't have any more private time with Bethany?"

"Yes."

Lucy nodded. "Just as I thought."

"What?"

"You're as crazy in love with her as she is with you."

Nash didn't have anything to say to that. His mother was right about him, and he suspected she was right about Bethany. It didn't matter. They'd both suck it up and deal.

As Bethany had known it would, Opal's arrival changed everything. Because Opal was determined to be there if the *Real News* crew showed up, Bethany checked with Nash and got the okay to offer Opal the king bed. Her chauffeur produced a small suitcase from the back of the limo and Opal changed into a slacks outfit and flats. It was as casual as Opal ever got, but it allowed her to roam around and talk to the work crew.

Bethany should have known she'd do that. She was the most social person Bethany had ever known, which was why being a talk show host was perfect for her. She soon had everyone eating out of her hand.

By the end of the day, the ranch had been transformed into the picture postcard Opal had predicted when she'd arrived. The outbuildings were painted Barn Red with white trim. The exterior of the ranch house had been stained gray, so that its trendy weathered look now appeared to be on purpose. The front steps no longer creaked, and even the plumbing had been tamed, at least a little bit.

After Lucy's remark, Bethany expected Opal to ask about Nash, but she didn't. Bethany took her cue from that and made sure she remained friendly but distant whenever she happened to be around Nash, which wasn't often. She wondered if that was his plan.

Sarah hosted a huge dinner at the Last Chance that night, and although Bethany hoped for at least one moment alone with Nash, it never came. Sarah offered Opal's chauffeur a room at the Last Chance, but all he would accept was a sleeping bag he could put on the sofa of Bethany's living room at the Triple G.

That was when Bethany figured out Emile had been hired as Opal's bodyguard and could probably do many things besides drive a limo. Now that she understood his role, she noticed that his cell phone was hardly ever out of his hand. For all she knew, he had reinforcements standing at the ready if Opal's safety was ever in question.

Once Bethany had driven Opal and Emile back to the Triple G in her rented SUV, she wondered if Opal would grab an opportunity for a woman-to-woman chat, either in the kitchen or out on the front porch. But she claimed exhaustion from jet lag and went straight to bed.

The following morning, *Real News* showed up, but they'd sent a skeleton crew. They must have been tipped off that there really wasn't much of a story, and besides, Opal was there. Nobody messed with Opal Knightly unless they wanted to tank their ratings. She was beloved.

Once the news van pulled out of the yard, Opal turned to Bethany. "Well, honey, I guess that's it. Ready to come home to Atlanta with me?" Her green gaze was steady.

"Now?" Somehow Bethany hadn't expected that, but she should have. Opal traveled by private jet, and it would be parked at the Jackson airport with the pilot waiting for departure instructions.

Opal shrugged. "Might as well. The disaster's been averted, thanks to your friends."

"And you." She smiled at her benefactor. "The *Real News* reporters weren't about to get nasty with you standing there. Thank you for coming."

"You're welcome. But I do have to get back, and so do you, for that matter. You don't have to be here for the closing. That can all be handled with faxes and such. And my private jet is a lot more comfortable than any commercial flight. We can head over to the Last Chance in your little SUV and say goodbye to whoever's around while Emile makes his tortuous way down that awful road. Then we can drive tandem to Jackson."

She spoke with the implicit authority of someone who'd built a multimillion-dollar career with nothing more than guts and raw talent. She didn't expect objections, and Bethany wasn't about to give her any. "Sure, we can do that. I'll pack."

"And that's the other advantage. I'm sure you have a few boxes of things you want to take, mementos and such. I don't charge for extra luggage." She flashed her Opal smile.

As Bethany rushed around for the next hour packing up, she decided that Opal was doing her a favor and might even know that. Hanging around another day or two would only prolong the agony of leaving. A woman who'd achieved Opal's level of success would believe in ripping the bandage off quickly.

After loading everything into the SUV, Bethany locked the doors for the last time. She made sure Opal was buckled in and then drove away without looking back.

"That's that," Opal said. "Time to start a new story."

"Right." Bethany gripped the wheel, swallowed the lump in her throat and concentrated on getting down the road without jostling her famous passenger any more than necessary.

All the way over to the Last Chance, Opal chatted easily about Bethany's planned segment—sprinkled with insider jokes about recent guests who'd appeared on the show—and whether or not the Atlanta Braves had a chance to win the pennant. Bethany made a few comments, but she was glad Opal didn't expect her to be a brilliant conversationalist. Fortunately with Opal, that wasn't necessary.

As they pulled into the circular gravel drive in front of the ranch house, Bethany glanced around, hoping for a glimpse of Nash. She didn't see him. She and Opal climbed the steps and rang the doorbell.

Sarah answered the door with surprised delight and invited them in. "Did the *Real News* crew show up?"

"They did," Opal said. "And they got next to nothing. Your help was invaluable. Thank you for that."

"Yes," Bethany added. "The place looks fabulous."

"I'm glad it worked out." Sarah gestured toward the living room. "Come on in. I'll have Mary Lou bring us coffee."

"I wish we could stay for coffee," Opal said. "But we're on the way to the airport."

"Oh! Well, of course. I'm sure you're a very busy lady. But you're coming back after that, right, Bethany?"

"No, I'm afraid not. I'm leaving with Opal."

Sarah's smile faded. "I thought you might stay on a few more days. We're just getting acquainted."

"I know." There was that lump in her throat again. "But this makes sense. I have plenty of things I need to do in Atlanta, and I can take my boxes of keepsakes in Opal's plane instead of trusting them to the airlines."

Sarah nodded. "I suppose you're right. Are you sure you can't stay for coffee, though? I'm the only one here right now, but I could call and see where some of the others are. I'm sure they'll want to say goodbye if they can make it over."

"I'm sorry as all get-out, but we have to be moving on," Opal said. "It's a long flight and I have to tape a show in the morning."

"All right, then. It was wonderful to meet you." She shook Opal's hand. Then she turned to Bethany. "Any messages you want me to convey?"

"Do you...? Could I borrow a piece of paper?"

"Sure. Hang on a minute." Sarah hurried into the office and returned quickly with a white notepad and a pen.

Heart racing, Bethany took it, aware of Opal waiting for her. But she had to leave Nash some small note, even if she had no idea what to say. Finally she scribbled out "Nash, I'll never forget you. Bethany."

She didn't dare sign it *with love.* That would be cruel. She folded the note and handed it to Sarah. "Please give this to Nash, and...let everyone know how much I appreciate what they did. It was..." She couldn't go on.

"I'll tell them." Sarah gave her a quick hug. "Safe travels, you two."

Bethany had thought leaving the Triple G was tough, but driving away from the Last Chance felt as if she'd amputated a limb. She vaguely remembered driving to the airport. After that, Opal's people took over.

As the sleek jet rose into the clear blue of a Wyoming summer day, she closed her eyes and fought to keep from breaking down. This would be the hardest part. Surely she couldn't hurt this much forever.

NASH MOVED INTO THE house at the Triple G, but he couldn't make himself sleep in the king bed. Instead he slept in Bethany's little twin because it smelled the most like her and had more memories attached to it. The bed didn't fit him very well, but that didn't matter because he wasn't sleeping much, anyway.

Three long weeks passed. Every day he worked at the Last Chance until he was exhausted, and then he drove to the Triple G and worked some more until he was catatonic. Jack loaned him a horse, and sometimes he'd take Tie-Dye out for long rides, hoping the spectacular scenery and fresh air would help. Other times he drank too much beer, hoping that would help.

Nothing really did. He had lost the love of his life, and he wasn't sure how he would manage to get over that. The pain was a hundred times worse than when he'd ended his marriage to Lindsay. That had been a relationship doomed from the start.

Bethany wasn't Lindsay. She focused on people, not things, and she would never allow income, either his or hers, to be a bone of contention between them. But that lovely little insight didn't help ease the pain. Because he loved her, he wanted her to have this amazing opportunity. And somehow, he'd learn to survive.

He'd formed the habit of sitting on the back stoop to catch the view of the Tetons at sunset. He always took a beer, her parting note and his phone, not that he got that many calls. He hadn't been the best company lately, and his friends and family must have figured out he wanted to be left alone for a while. The celebration he'd planned to have at the Spirits and Spurs after closing on the ranch had never happened.

But tonight, for some reason, his phone rang, and it was an area code and number he didn't recognize. He swered, expecting someone wanting him to answer survey questions.

A crisp voice came on the line. "Please hold for Opal Knightly."

"Opal Knightly?" Nash straightened so fast he almost fell off the stoop.

"Yes, sir. Please hold."

Nash set his beer carefully on the step beside him, tucked Bethany's note in his left shirt pocket and took a deep breath. He couldn't imagine what this was about, but Opal Knightly was an efficient and busy woman who didn't make idle phone calls.

"Nash Bledsoe?" The rich voice made him think of her day in Jackson Hole, which made him think of Bethany, which made him hurt like hell.

"Yes. How can I help you, Opal?"

"I'll cut to the chase. Bethany is miserable without you. I thought she'd come around, but the girl seems to be so deep in love she can't see straight, which presents a problem."

Nash's chest grew tight. He wasn't sure whether that came from joy that Bethany missed him or sorrow because she wasn't happy. "What do you want from me?"

"Do you love her back?"

"Yes, of course I do, but—"

"Then I can work with you. If you'd said no, I'd have sent her to counseling and maybe a spa. But since you love her, here's the plan. I like it, and I think she likes it, although she keeps blathering on about being ungrateful for what I've done for her. But mostly she doesn't think you'll like it, at least not yet."

He did his best to breathe, but it was difficult. "Does she know you're calling me?"

"No. She'd have a fit. She insists you need time settle in, maybe a year or so, before you'd be ready hear about this plan. But I hate to see the girl spen year being miserable."

"I hate to think of her spending a minute being m erable. What's the plan?"

"Well." Opal took a breath. "I've finally realize she's not cut out for the talk show gig. She's more an introvert who's happier writing, but she also enjoy working with people when she's out of the spotlight. suggested that the Triple G would make a great retre for stressed-out CEOs. You'd have to build cottage for them, get some horses, take 'em out riding, and yo could handle all that. Bethany could write her book and counsel the CEOs in a lovely setting. You'd bot make a good living."

"You mean she'd live here full-time?" The idea dazzled him, but he dared not believe in it.

"She would, but she doesn't think you'll like this idea of mine, which would change how the ranch is utilized. And you own the place, so it's your call. What do you think?"

"Opal, I would cut off my right arm for that woman. If she could be happy here counseling stressed-out CEOs and writing her books, I would do anything to make that happen."

"I'm glad to hear you say that. Here's what you can do for me, then. Come on the show day after tomorrow and propose to her on the air."

"What?" His heart kicked into a full gallop.

"Can you do that? I'll send my private plane to the Jackson airport tomorrow. My people will see that you have a hotel room and are fed, and they'll advise you

n clothes, but the cowboy look is good. The audience
will love that. Oh, and get a ring."

Nash opened his mouth, but nothing came out.

"Nash, honey, are you there? Or did you pass out?"

He sucked in air. "I'm here."

"Will you do it?"

The way he saw it, he had no choice. If he wanted
Bethany, this was how he'd get her. "Yes, I'll do it."

SOMETHING WAS UP. BETHANY could tell from the extra
sparkle in Opal's green eyes as she and her mentor fiddled with their mikes and did a sound check. Normally
Bethany's segment was at the end of the show, but for
some reason Opal wanted her to lead off today.

The studio audience seemed especially lively this
morning, too, as if they knew something that Bethany
didn't. She leaned toward Opal. "You have something
up your sleeve, don't you?"

Opal smiled as the opening theme song played.
"Ready?"

"I hope so. You know I don't like surprises, right?"

"So you've told me." The talk show host faced the
camera as the director counted down the seconds. Then
she put on what Bethany called her *Opal face* and began
her monologue, touching on a few current events and
the latest Atlanta Braves game.

Next, she introduced Bethany's segment, but instead
of leaving Bethany to handle it alone, she stayed on the
set. "I'm sticking around for this one." She winked at
the audience.

Bethany's stomach churned with dread. She hated
surprises, and she hated them even more on live television.

Opal smiled at her with normal good cheer. "As we all know, Bethany, you've inspired thousands of people to believe in your mantra and choose happiness instead of pain."

Bethany focused on breathing normally. "It's rewarding to think that I've had that effect."

"Oh, you definitely have. We've had many testimonials, both in person and from viewers calling in. But I thought it would be special for our audience to watch someone in the process of choosing happiness over pain, right here, right now, in real time. Are you up for that?"

Oh, God. What now? "Of course. That's always a wonderful moment."

"Then welcome today's special guest, Nash Bledsoe."

Bethany gasped and felt the blood drain from her face. "Nash is here?"

"I am." He walked onto the set, the heels of his polished boots clicking on the floor. The black jeans, white shirt and black hat appeared new, but they fit him as if they were custom-made. He looked like a million bucks. "Hello, Bethany."

She popped out of her chair and then wished she hadn't, because she was a little dizzy. "What are you doing here?"

He caught her elbow and steadied her. He had a mike clipped to his shirt. "Choosing happiness."

She put a hand over her mike because she could hear herself gasping for breath, which did nothing for her cool and professional image, either.

"I love you." He said the words loud and clear, without a single waver. "I choose to be happy with you."

The audience let out a collective sigh, but all Bethany ould do was stare at him in disbelief.

Covering his own mike, he leaned forward and mur- ured in her ear. "I love Opal's plan. Just go along with is, okay? Then we can get out of here."

Her heart hammered wildly. This was happening. It asn't a dream. "You're being bossy, Nash."

"I'm a little agitated, okay? Just follow my lead. Please."

As Bethany took a long, shaky breath, it all became clear. Opal was setting her free so that she could live the life she wanted with Nash. But being Opal, she al- ways had her eye on the ratings. A stunt like this would send them through the roof. After all Opal had done for her, Bethany couldn't begrudge her a ratings boost.

Taking another deep breath, she looked into Nash's blue eyes and saw the love shining there. He'd agreed to this drama because Opal had asked him and he knew how much Opal meant to her. If he could go along with it, so could she. She gave a subtle nod.

With that, Nash dropped to one knee, reached into his shirt pocket and pulled out a diamond ring that glit- tered under the studio lights. "Will you marry me, Beth- any Grace? Will you choose to be happy with me?"

She cleared her throat, uncovered her mike and smiled down at him. "Because I love you with all my heart, my answer is *yes*."

The audience erupted.

Holding her gaze, Nash slipped the ring on her fin- ger. Then he rose to his feet, tossed his hat into the au- dience and gave her a kiss that blocked out everything. When he finally lifted his head, the cheers and whistles deafened her.

"Give them a big send-off!" Opal called out. "Be cause they're leaving before this show becomes too ho for daytime television!"

Nash hurried Bethany offstage. A crew membe quickly divested them of their mikes.

Bethany turned to Nash. "What now?"

"Opal has a limo outside waiting for us."

"And then? What happens after that?"

He grinned at her as he took her hand and pulled her toward the exit. "Our future, which is gonna be great."

"Is that a promise?" She really didn't have to ask. Nash was a man of his word.

He stopped. Slowly he turned to her and cupped her face in his big hands. "Yes, it's a promise." His voice was gruff with emotion as his unwavering gaze held hers. "I cross my heart."

Epilogue

As the cowhands enjoyed their usual predawn breakfast in the bunkhouse, Emmett made an appearance. Luke Griffin wasn't surprised to see the foreman show up. Yesterday had been Nash's final day of work at the Last Chance, so logically Emmett would need to reassign Nash's former duties.

Nash had already asked Luke if he'd be interested in a job over at the Triple G, but Luke had respectfully declined. Normally he got itchy feet after a year or so of being in an area, and he'd likely leave Jackson Hole in a few months. No point in hiring on with Nash for such a short time, much as he liked the guy and wished the best for both Nash and Bethany. Luke was a rolling stone and didn't anticipate that changing anytime soon.

As expected, Emmett discussed the changes Nash's departure would mean. He spread the extra work among all of them so no one was impacted too much, but Emmett also promised that someone would be hired to fill Nash's spot within the next month.

"One other thing." Emmett paused to refresh his cof-

fee. "I need to make you all aware of the eagle situa‑
tion."

"The nest is still there," a big-eared cowboy name
Danny said. "At least it was two days ago. And unles
I miss my guess, it's got eggs in it."

Emmett took a sip of his coffee. "Yes, it does. An
there's a young lady who's applied for a private gra
to study those eagles and their chicks, assuming th
eggs hatch."

"Who's that?" asked a lanky redheaded cowhand
named Jeb.

"Naomi Perkins."

"Oh, yeah." Jeb nodded. "I remember her. Worked
for her folks at the diner before she went off to college.
She's back, then?"

"Yep. Lost her job with Game and Fish in Florida.
So this grant would help her out, and since the nest is
on Last Chance property, Jack's given her permission to
be out there to study them if the grant comes through.
Just wanted all of you to be aware."

"So what does she look like?" Luke asked, and im‑
mediately everybody started ribbing him. "Hey!" he
shouted over the general uproar. "I need to know so I
can identify her!"

"Yeah, right," Danny said. "You want to know if it's
worth riding out there and striking up a conversation."

"I don't know what she looks like now," Jeb said.
"She was kind of cute before, blonde, blue eyes, but
you never know. People change. Has anybody seen her
since she came back?"

"Jack has, I guess," Emmett said. "But it doesn't
matter what she looks like. I'm sure if any of you see a

onde up in a tree in the general area where the eagles
e nesting, you'll figure out it's her."

Luke had to smile at that. "Good point. We don't have
o many tree-climbing blondes at the Last Chance."
nd he was intrigued. He'd never met a woman who
ade her living studying wild creatures. Naomi Per-
ns, eagle watcher, sounded like someone he should
t to know.

* * * * *

#755 WILD AT HEART • *Sons of Chance*
by Vicki Lewis Thompson

A degree in wildlife management hasn't prepared
Naomi Perkins for the challenge of taming a gorgeous cowboy
like Luke Griffin. But she's going to have a lot of fun trying!

#756 LEAD ME ON
by Crystal Green

Bridesmaid Margot Walker has a wonderful idea to raise money
for her friend's wedding—putting a basket full of spicy date
ideas up for auction. She's hoping her college crush buys it.
Too bad her archenemy, Clint Barrows, beats him to it...

#757 FREE FALL • *Uniformly Hot!*
by Karen Foley

The last thing Maggie Copeland expects to find when she
returns to the small hometown she fled ten years ago is a man
who makes her want to stay...

#758 SHE'S NO ANGEL
by Kira Sinclair

Architect Brett Newcomb has always had a sweet tooth, but he
might have bitten off more than he can chew with chocolatier
Lexi Harper...
